A ravaged tomorrow, a planet in ruins, sent a lone agent back to save the past—now. But Bill Johnson found our world facing a host of crises, not just one.

Nuclear annihilation. Terrorism. Tyranny. Pollution. Population. Plague. Famine. Each menace Johnson solved simply set the stage for the next, an endless clip of bullets springing before the firing pin.

Johnson was forced to save the world, again—and again—and again—

And whenever time changed, tomorrow—shifted. Until Johnson was lost, a hero with no home, no friend, no memory. He had only visions and a helpless destiny to find the worst troublespots on Earth. Johnson wasn't just trapped in the past—he was trapped in the future.

All futures.

CRISIS!

JAMES GUNN

CRISIS!

A TOM DOHERTY ASSOCIATES BOOK

This is a work of fiction. All the characters and events portrayed in this book are fictional, and any resemblance to real people or incidents is purely coincidental.

CRISIS!

Copyright © 1986 by James Gunn

All rights reserved, including the right to reproduce this book or portions thereof in any form.

First printing: May 1986

A TOR Book

Published by Tom Doherty Associates
49 West 24 Street
New York, N.Y. 10010

Cover art by Janny Wurts

ISBN: 0-812-53944-3
CAN. ED.: 0-812-53945-1

Printed in the United States

0 9 8 7 6 5 4 3 2 1

ACKNOWLEDGMENTS

"Child of the Sun" was first published in *Analog*, March 1978.

"End of the World" was first published in *Analog*, January 1984.

"Man of the Hour" was first published in *Analog*, October 1984.

"Touch of the Match" was first published in *Analog*, March 1985.

"Woman of the Year" was first published in *Analog*, April 1985.

"Will-of-the-Wisp" was first published in *Analog*, May 1985.

To
Ben Bova and Stanley Schmidt,
editors of vision

Contents

Prelude:
Man in the Cage   11

Episode One:
End of the World   13

Episode Two:
Child of the Sun   45

Episode Three:
Man of the Hour   83

Episode Four:
Touch of the Match   125

Episode Five:
Woman of the Year   155

Episode Six:
Will-of-the-Wisp   189

Prelude
Man in the Cage

He never knew whether he was troubled by memory or nightmare.

Every few days he dreamed about a pendulum. It swung back and forth like the regulator of a clock. He sensed the movement and he heard a sound, not a tick but a swoosh, as if something were moving rapidly through the air. At first he had only a vague impression of things, but gradually details came into focus. The pendulum arm, for instance, was more like a silvery chain with wires running through it down to the weight at the end.

Then scale became apparent. The entire apparatus was big. It swung in a cavern whose sides were so distant they could not be seen, and the wires were thick, like bus bars. The weight was a kind of cage, and it was large enough to hold a person standing upright. Somewhere, far beyond the cavern, unpleasantness waited. Here, there was only hushed expectancy.

In his dream he could see only the glittering chain and the cage; it swung back and forth, and at the end of each swing, where the pendulum should have slowed before it started its return, the cage blurred as if it were swinging too fast to be seen.

At this point he always realized that the cage was occupied. He was in the cage. And he understood that the pendulum marked not the passage of time but a passage through time.

The dream always ended the same way: the cage arrived with a barely perceptible jar, with a cessation of motion, and he woke up. Even awake he had the sense that somewhere the pendulum still was swinging, he still was in the cage, and eyes were watching him—or perhaps a single eye, like a camera, that revealed to him a scene of what might be. . . .

Episode One
End of the World

He was lying on his right side, his right leg drawn up, his right arm stretched out, his left arm lying along his side and hip. Another wide bed was beside him, its slick, dark-green spread unwrinkled, its pillow-bulges intact against the dark wood of the headboard. Beyond the bed was a small desk with a straight chair in front of it. To its left was a six-sided pedestal table made of dark wood; armchairs on wheels and covered with green plastic stood on either side. Beyond that was a window sealed from the outer light or dark by heavy drapes and curtains, but a line like bright silver ascended vertically where they failed to meet.

The man rose to a sitting position, his knees drawn up. A television set stood in the corner, its large blank eye challenging him to fill it with pictures and meaning. A dresser with two sets of three drawers was against the wall at the foot of the beds, above it a wide mirror. The room was standard hotel. Farther to the left would be a bathroom with a tub that could be turned into a shower by closing a curtain or plastic doors, a stool, and a broad, imitation-marble lavatory with a mirror above. If this were a better-than-average hotel, the bathroom would have an anteroom with an open closet facing a wet bar; on the bar would be a plastic tub, which could be filled with ice from a machine down the hall, and four plastic glasses sealed into polyethylene bags.

All of this the man should have known but didn't. Instead he swung his legs over the edge of the bed and stretched his arms high above his head in an instinctive gesture of loosening sleep-tightened muscles. When he stood up, he was of medium height. He was pleasant looking, but nothing more, and slender; he had brown, curly hair and dark eyes and skin that looked evenly tanned. He gazed around him with the innocent absorption of a newly born infant and then his eyes stopped at a slip of white paper stuck to the right-hand side of the dresser mirror. He stood up and looked at it. "Read the letter in the top right-hand drawer," it said.

The man stood naked in front of the mirror and looked down at the drawer as if he didn't want to open it. Finally he moved his hand forward and pulled on the handle. A long white envelope lay just inside the drawer, crosswise, the return address of a hotel on its upper left-hand corner. The man reached into the drawer and removed the envelope. He tore it open. Inside were two sheets of hotel stationery with black hand-lettering on them.

"Your name is Bill Johnson," they read. "You have just saved the U.S. space program from termination, and you don't remember. You can find references to the political decisions in newspapers and magazines, but you will find no mention of the part you played.

"For this there are several possible explanations, including the likelihood I may be lying or deceived or insane. But the explanation on which you must act is that I have told you the truth: you are a man born in a future that has almost used up all hope; you were sent to this time and place to alter the events that created that future.

"Am I telling the truth? The only evidence you have is your apparently unique ability to foresee consequences—it comes like a vision, not of the future because the future can be changed, but of what will happen if events take their natural course, if someone does not act, if you do not intervene.

"But each time you intervene, no matter how subtly, you change the future from which you came. You exist in this time and outside of time and in the future, and so each change makes you forget.

"I wrote this letter last night to tell you what I know, just as I learned about myself a few weeks ago in a similar manner, for I am you and we are one, and we have done this many times before. . . ."

The letter was signed "Bill Johnson."

The man in the room found a pen on the desk and wrote "Bill Johnson" under the name on the letter. The signatures looked identical. He took the letter into the bathroom, tore it into small pieces, let the pieces flutter into the toilet bowl, and flushed them away. After he had finished showering—he did not need to shave—he collected a few toilet articles in a small plastic bag he found on the lavatory, and brought them to the dresser. The drawers were empty. In an imitation-leather suitcase resting on a rack beside the dresser he found clean underwear.

A shirt, a jacket, and a pair of pants were hanging in the closet. He put the clothing on along with the brown shoes that were on the closet floor.

In the pocket of the coat he found a billfold; in the billfold were one hundred forty-three dollars, a Visa charge card, and a plastic-encased social security card. The last two bore the name of Bill Johnson. On the dresser were a few coins, a key attached to a red plastic hotel medallion, and a black pocket comb. He put them in his pants pockets.

Finally he faced the cyclopean stare of the television set in the corner and twisted and pulled the knobs until he found the one that turned it on. In a moment the screen was filled with the face of a news announcer, replaced occasionally by films and maps, but the controlled hysteria of the announcer's voice continued without interruption or variety, except when his voice and face were replaced by those of other reporters equally panicky and equally professional.

Johnson listened and watched for half an hour, sitting on the edge of the bed, occasionally looking as if he were seeing more than appeared on the front of the glass tube. Finally he turned the set off, went to the dresser, picked up his suitcase, and walked to the door. He looked back. Except for the unmade bed and the imprint of his body on the side of the other, both of which soon would be removed, the room bore no trace of his existence.

He walked down the carpeted hallway, his footsteps as distant as the future, into the broad lobby. Sunlight slanted brilliantly through the distant glass doors, but reached only a few feet into the space. Elsewhere a subdued lighting from scattered lamps set by overstuffed chairs and sofas almost disguised the fact that the lobby was deserted.

At the front desk a dark-haired clerk who looked to be

of draft age was listening to a portable radio. "Soviet forces continue to assemble at the Iranian border near the Soviet city of Ashkhabad and the Afghanistan city of Herat. The President has placed the U.S. military forces on full alert. Aircraft-carrier task forces are steaming at top speed toward the Arabian Sea from bases in the Pacific, and the Mediterranean fleet has put out from bases in Italy. Rumors persist that the President has been on the hotline to Moscow several times, but that mounting threats rather than conciliation have been the only result. . . ."

Johnson tapped on the desk with his hotel key, and the clerk, noticing him for the first time, gave an apologetic smile. "Sorry," he said. "People have a hard time keeping their mind on business these days."

"I know."

"You're checking out?"

"Bill Johnson," he said.

The clerk leafed through a metal file and drew out a bill. "You're paid up," he said.

"May the future be kind," Johnson said, and picked up his bag and walked through the lobby into the blinding sunlight.

The nearby airport was packed with people twitching like a netful of newly caught mackerel. Lines jiggled in front of every airline counter. People moved from one to another as the fortunes of one line moved it forward and difficult problems or difficult customers delayed another.

Johnson took his place in one line and remained patiently in it as the line slowly moved forward to break against the counter like a wave in slow motion. Words of protest and pleading and anger reached Johnson as he neared the front. The man and woman just ahead of him took a long time insisting that they had to get home, that they had children there and they had to get them out of town before the bombs fell, that they had tickets assuring them of a place on this flight. The ticket agent was blond and round-faced and a sweater. In other times he might have been jolly and sympathetic, but now he was frowning, and sweat gathered on his forehead and ran down the wrinkles and dripped on the counter while he explained with a calm close to fury that military passengers had first priority, that the government had recalled every military person on leave and called up everyone from the Reserve, and that the airline would get them the first available seats.

When he reached the head of the line, Johnson put down his small suitcase and said quietly, "That's good enough for me—the first available seat to New York." He handed over his credit card. His actions and words were like the first layer of pearl around an irritant.

The agent looked at him incredulously and then his anger began to leak away. He laughed. "There may be a special flight out of here about four in the morning. Otherwise it may be tomorrow night before I can get you onto anything."

"Whatever you can do. I'll wait as long as necessary."

The agent laughed again. "You're the kind of customer I can do business with, Mr. . . ." he looked at the credit card, ". . . Johnson. We really shouldn't accept credit cards, you know. If the bombs drop there could be an electromagnetic pulse, an EMP, that could wipe out all the computer records in the country."

"If the bombs drop, money and checks won't be much better," Johnson said lightly. "You have to go on as if disaster weren't going to happen. That's our only chance of preventing it."

The agent looked thoughtful. "That's right," he said. The line was stirring impatiently, and some customers were complaining to the air around them at the nerve of some people and the chitchat when everybody else was in a life-and-death hurry, forgetting that they, in their turn, would take as long as they considered necessary. The agent tapped his computer keys, made out a charge slip, and handed ticket and charge slip to Johnson. "No use asking you smoking or non-smoking. That's a luxury we can't afford any more," the agent said while Johnson was signing the charge slip and recovering his charge card. "Maybe it's illegal, but who's going to check up?"

Johnson picked up his ticket and his suitcase and turned away. "May the future be kind," he said.

"Yeah," the agent replied before turning to the next desperate customer.

The rest of the day, except for a few visits to the restaurant, the water fountain, and the men's room, Johnson spent staring out the broad windows at the airport runways. He did not stare the way the others did, like grackles turning their mad yellow eyes toward a falling sky, but like a member of the audience who knows when the curtain will fall.

Airplanes taxied to the head of runways like crippled albatrosses and sat for minutes that turned into hours as they waited their turn. More airplanes descended from the sky and sandpapered their tires across broad concrete before bellowing to speeds slow enough to turn onto ramps. Then the first airplane in line would swing onto the runway and start accelerating before quite lined up and then, gathering speed, lift its improbable nose into the air, and the giant weight of the great machine would follow, and it would climb.

One would arrive and one depart, and then two would arrive and one depart, then two depart and one arrive, persistently, hypnotically, interminably. The sky was cloudless and blue as if it had no thoughts different from the ones it had mused upon for eons past, of birds and clouds and smoke, of rain and hail and sleet and snow.

During the daytime the crowds of people clumped together, their luggage deposited around them like megaliths, and talked, at first agitated and then, as anger faded, in bitterness and fear. Others, isolated in cocoons of individual concerns, listened to radios or sat in front of television screens in the bars, drawing their eyes away only to order another round. Some competed for the chairs that were never planned for such a multitude; some stood or sat on their bags or settled on the floor where they could lean against the wall. Some fell asleep.

Troops in khaki and blue and green marched into the terminal and then stood around, smoking cigarettes and feigning nonchalance until ushered first through metal detectors into waiting airplanes; then civilians surged forward, tickets clutched high in one hand, bags held in the other, all but a lucky few to be turned back by sweating airline personnel. Some left the terminal in discouragement, but always more came until gradually, as night fell, the numbers dwindled as some gave up and others drifted toward nearby motels or homes.

By night the terminal had assumed a different character. The coming and going airplanes were more mysterious and less fascinating; they appeared out of nothing preceded by lights glaring like the eyes of mad giants, and disappeared into nothing, leaving only their thunder behind. The lights in the terminal ceiling far overhead could not replace the sunlight that had streamed through the windows, and people turned to each other, spoke to strangers, confided their problems.

Talking about the terrifying uncertainty of attack, confessing why they had come to this distant place and why they had to get back, laying out their plans for what they would do when they got where they were going, how they would survive the bombs and how they would survive after the bombs, none mentioning the possibility of surrender, none of them repeating the cowardly statement that the living would envy the dead, all of them sure that living, if only for a few more days or a few more hours, was worthwhile, speaking most of all to the man with the curly brown hair and the dark eyes that looked as if they had seen too much for one so young. For he listened, listened while engines roared in the night like carnivorous jungle animals, listened to confidences and revelations in the sterile light of fixtures embedded in concrete beams high above, listened without judging, listened with occasional sounds of sympathy. . . .

. . . Listened to an older man in uniform who had been called back into service as a member of the reserve, complaining that he had been assured that those in the reserve, because they already had been trained, would be called after everybody else, reflecting that with the potential for worldwide destruction it might not matter whether a person was in the service or at home, shaking his head at the folly of war but his voice hardening when he spoke of the cruelty and barbarity of "the enemy," he who had been through one war already, but smiling, finally, with the relief of feeling that it was going to be all right anyway.

. . . Listened to a boy in marine green, his blond hair still cut only half an inch from his pink scalp, just out of boot camp and now, home only three days of a fourteen-day leave and enjoying the admiration of more than one girlfriend, called to rejoin his unit for the real thing, excited, fingers twitching, shoulders jerking, speculating about the thrilling uncertainty ahead, enjoying the anticipation of war, saying that his guys would show them how to fight.

. . . Listened to a teen-aged girl who had come out here to visit relatives for the summer but now must hurry back to her family so that they could survive—or die—together, depressed and animated in turn, talking about the horrors and insanity of war and her plans for the future as if they could coexist, referring as nastily as she could to the nasty enemy, looking at the boys in uniform with wide, speculative eyes, blushing at their ribald invitations but enjoying them, too.

. . . Listened to an older man, maybe forty-five or fifty, with eyes gray and deep, here to look for work but now returning to his home to die, if it came to that, where he had lived, talking about success and failure and how it didn't matter any more, and if he were younger he would join up and fight the bastards, as if it would be hand-to-hand combat, but maybe it didn't matter anyway, and the people who died in the city were just as important as the people who pushed buttons that shot weapons.

. . . Listened to an old woman who had been born in Europe, her face lined with memories, talking with resignation about the dream that was turning to ashes.

. . . Listened to a young sailor who had just raped a girl, only it wasn't really rape, just a shortage of time.

And measured their guilts and their dreams, their fears and their courage.

And absolved them.

And that was the end of the first day.

* * *

After the fever of the airports—LaGuardia pulsed at an even higher level—Manhattan was cool. An unbroken stream of traffic was leaving the island on all the bridges and through all the tunnels, and almost no traffic was entering. People moved warily; nobody spoke to anyone else, but occasionally an accidental jostle turned to screams and even blows. And yet the island was calm; people went about their jobs purposefully or fatalistically. But there were fewer of them, and this reduced the pressure.

Johnson checked into the anonymity of the New York Hilton. There was no line at the registration desk and few people loitered in the lobby. The restaurants were almost deserted, even though it was breakfast time.

About ten in the morning Johnson walked the three short blocks to the Associated Press Building in Rockefeller Center and took the elevator to the editorial offices. He told the receptionist that he wanted to see the managing editor. "She's busy right now," the young man said. He was tall and dark and not particularly good-looking, but he had an expressive face. Right now it expressed suspicion. "May I tell her your name and the business you want to discuss?"

"Bill Johnson," Johnson said and smiled without showing his teeth. The receptionist's apprehension eased. "And the business I have is how to stop a war."

The receptionist looked at him as if speculating how soon to call Bellevue, but Johnson sat down peacefully in a chair beside an end table with a tall lamp on it, and the receptionist looked away. Johnson picked up a copy of the Associated Press annual report and found that the name of the managing editor was Frances Miller. After half an hour of reading balance sheets, Johnson was ushered into a big office. In it was a big desk made of some dark wood that gleamed in the sunlight coming through a window that looked out upon Rockefeller Plaza. Beside the desk was a computer terminal. Facing it were a couple of armchairs covered in brown leather, and against the right wall was a matching sofa. Several framed pictures adorned paneled walls.

The woman behind the desk did not look like a managing editor or a Frances. She was cool and blonde and beautiful in a gray jacket and skirt and white blouse, but her eyes were gray and hard as if too many people had tried to talk her into too many things. "I understand you want to stop a war," she said. She looked at the LED time display on her desk. "I'm trying to report one, and I'm busier than you can imagine. You've got two minutes to convince me that I ought to take more than that."

"I've got just six days to stop this war," he said evenly, and sat down on the front of the chair facing the desk, "and two minutes to convince you to help me." He held out his hands as if measuring something in front of him. "I have visions of the future."

"Ninety seconds," she said.

"In five seconds your phone is going to ring, and an assistant editor is going to ask if he can release a bulletin—"

The woman's eyes had switched to the time display. As the five-second period elapsed, the telephone rang. After she put it down, she said, "That was a trick. You heard something when you came in, or saw people talking in the office as you came through."

"Your receptionist is going to knock at the door and ask if you need him. He means, of course, to help get rid of me."

After the receptionist went away Miller forgot to look at

CRISIS!

her time display again. Instead she looked at Johnson as if she saw him for the first time. "What kind of talent do you have?"

"I don't really see the future," he said, and when she started to speak he held up his right hand, palm up, in a gesture of explanation. "I see visions of what will happen if events take their natural course."

"Extrapolation."

"Yes, but more than just a guess."

"And what do you see now?" she asked, unable to keep a note of skepticism from creeping into her voice.

"Explosions. Flames. People dying. All over the world. Some quickly, vaporized in a fraction of a second. Some lingeringly. A world dying. Everything: animals, plants. I see an Earth as sterile as Venus."

"That's what everybody sees," she said.

"That's what everybody imagines," he corrected. "I *see* it."

His eyes were dark with knowledge and deep with anguish. She looked at them, and then, for the first time, turned her gaze away as if she saw a fellow human suffering and could not help.

"I can see individual tragedies. Your death, for instance."

She held up a slender white hand. "No thanks," she said, with a touch of irony. "I want to be surprised. You said you had a plan."

"I said that my business was how to stop a war. But I do have a plan." He leaned forward as if taking her into his confidence. "I don't blame you for being suspicious. Lots of people must want to use you, and anybody could walk off the street with a plan."

Some of her inherent skepticism seemed to fade from

her face. "It's just that you said you saw the world in flames."

"That's what will happen if events take their natural course." His voice was low and authoritative. "The future isn't fixed. I have personal knowledge of that. It can be changed. I hope to change it. I must change it."

The pain in his voice stopped her response for a moment. "How? I suppose the Associated Press plays a part in it?"

"You think this institution should not be used for someone else's purposes?"

"We're used all the time. But we don't do it knowingly unless it fits into our basic job."

"You make the news and people respond to it," he said.

"We just report what happens."

"Everything?"

"Of course."

"Everything?"

"Well, everything that is news."

"Is it news if you don't report it? I'm just a layman, but it seems to me that there is news you don't report in times like these."

"Like what?"

"News about the enemy that doesn't portray him as nasty, belligerent, murderous, treacherous, ignorant, despicable—"

"Stop!" she said, and smiled wryly. "There's some truth in that, but that's what people want to read."

"Oh," he said, "I thought you reported everything, not everything people wanted to read."

Her gaze came back to his eyes. "What do you want us to do?" She seemed weary suddenly, as if she had been sitting in that chair making too many decisions for too many hours.

"I can tell you what, but it would be better if you didn't know why. Maybe you can figure that out for yourself." When she seemed about to speak, he held up a hand. "But it doesn't betray your country or your profession."

"What is it?"

"If you could get out a few items here and there that make the enemy seem human—items about his daily life, his loving acts, his generosity, his sacrifices, his hopes and dreams and fears. . . ."

"I could get such items on the wire," she said, "but how could I get editors to print them or newscasters to broadcast them?"

"I'm not an expert in such matters," Johnson mused, "but I think I would assign them to someone very good, who would make the stories funny, dramatic, heartrending, witty—"

"You want us to use news as propaganda?"

"To use news as news. You don't have to invent the stories. They're happening. You aren't reporting them now. That's propaganda for war. Just find out about them and report them. Call it propaganda for peace, if you must, but it's really only complete reporting."

She studied his face. "You're giving me lessons in newspaper ethics." She paused and turned her chair to look out the window for a moment. When she turned back her face was decisive.

"Will it stop the war?"

"It's an indispensable part."

"Then it's worth a try." She straightened up and took a deep breath. "I feel ten years younger." She looked younger, now no longer forty but perhaps only in her early thirties. "What about the Russians? How are you going to get them to print happy news about us?"

"It isn't necessary. Their news is managed and so are their people. If the leaders want peace, there will be peace."

Frances Miller stood up, slender and elegant, and walked around her desk. Johnson stood up as she approached. She took his left hand and turned it over as if to look at the lines in his palm, but her eyes, no longer hard and suspicious, were looking at his face. "Before you came in," she said, "I would have bet a large amount that no one could talk me into anything this crazy."

"Why did you?"

"Maybe because you seem in so much pain. Who are you?"

"My name is Bill Johnson," he said.

She made a face. "The most common name in the telephone book in most cities. Where can I reach you if I need to?"

"I'm temporarily at the Hilton." He smiled. He was temporary everywhere.

"Who are you really?"

"I don't know," he said. "I woke up yesterday morning and didn't even know my name, only that something terrible was going to happen and that I had to stop it. I'm a man with no past and no future, only a compulsion."

"What else are you going to do?"

"I need information about computer experts," he said. "Can you help me with that?"

"I'll get our science reporter. If he can't help you, you can look through his files."

By noon Johnson had the name of the man he wanted.

* * *

The only problem was, the man was in jail.

At the penitentiary, the clerk, dark and sullen, said, "Tom Logan? What you want with him?"

"I need help."

"The kinda help he can give will put him back in jail. Maybe you, too."

"Back?"

"He was released a week ago. Served his time. Got a parole."

"You have an address?"

The clerk shook his head. "Against the rules."

"The name of his parole officer?"

"None of your business. The Russians are going to blow us up, or we're going to blow them up, or we're going to blow each other up, so what does it matter?"

"What would you like to have happen?"

"I'd like to see them blown right off this world," the clerk said, his upper lip raised to expose carnivorous canines.

"That's what I thought," Johnson said mildly and turned away.

On the rumbling train back to the city with sunlight still upon the hills and darkness in the Hudson River Valley, Johnson watched the green land and the rolling river as if they were something rare and infinitely valuable. The train had been full when it had gone north. Sailors and soldiers had been salted through the cars. Even the men's room had been crammed with people sitting on benches and seabags or on the floor, leaning against the wall and moving their legs out of the way when men wanted to use the lavatory or the toilet.

Now the train was almost empty, and the few people scattered among vacant seats did not want to be there and had no tolerance for idle conversation. They listened to radios through earplugs or read their newspapers, rattling the pages angrily as if somehow to exorcise the news or the enemy. Occasionally two people would be together, speaking in low voices, as if to be overheard was to reveal one's hopes to dark powers.

When Johnson got back to the hotel the night was late, the sky was overcast, and darkness was complete. A note waited for him to call Frances Miller. When he dialed the number she answered immediately.

"I thought you'd want to know," she said. "I've alerted our foreign correspondents, and the stories are coming in. I've got my best human-interest writer working on them, and the first of them ought to be out by morning. They think I'm crazy, you know."

"You're quite sane."

Her laughter was uneasy. "Sometimes I wonder."

"Only a crazy person would want to start a war. The people who want to stop one must be sane. You're working too hard. You're going to kill yourself."

She laughed. This time her voice was steadier. "Better me than a stranger. Are you on to anything?"

"I'll know tomorrow."

"If the world doesn't blow up first."

"We've got a few days left."

"How long?"

"You don't want to know."

"You're right. Knowing something like that would be terrible." There was a moment of silence as if she were recalling that he bore that terrible knowledge. "Your voice sounds different on the telephone."

"Everyone does."

"I know, but your voice sounds more . . . personal, as if I could tell you things."

"What do you want to tell me?"

"Oh"—she laughed—"nothing. Maybe some other time. Will we be in touch again?"

"I think so."

"Then good-bye for now."

"Good-bye."

She may have said something, but it was too soft to be heard. A moment later the telephone clicked and the dial tone began.

That was the end of the second day.

In the morning the world looked brighter. The clouds had parted and blue skies roofed the city's concrete corridors. The tension in the streets had dropped a level as if the barometer determined the likelihood of war.

Johnson's first stop was the building that housed the state department of probation and parole. There he learned that paperwork on recent parolees was a month behind, but he got a nearly illegible mimeographed list of local parole offices. He bought a cheap ballpoint pen at a discount drugstore and went through the list slowly, meditatively, checking locations in blue upon occasion. He ended up with thirteen marks. Methodically he began visiting offices.

Only one in three parole officers were in their office when he asked for them. Secretaries made excuses. "He'll be in later." "He's on a case." "She's on vacation." But some said sourly, "He's never in before noon" or "Stick around and we'll both be surprised." But everyone, secretaries and parole officers alike, shook their heads when he mentioned the name of Tom Logan. Finally, at the twelfth office, a perky, dark-haired secretary said, "I think the bum's skipped town, but he might have told me." And then, "Yeah, I remember Tom Logan. He reported here about a week ago. I noticed him particularly because he was too young-looking—too young to be a con, you know? Like a kid. No, the jerk locked up the files and took the keys. Like how am I supposed to get the work done around here?" After a thoughtful pause in which she appraised the figure and face of the man standing in front of her, she said quickly, "I do remember one thing. He had a job with a computer firm. I don't remember which one."

"But that's why he was sent to prison," Johnson said.

"I guess he was. Well, they don't give me reasons."

"Thanks, anyway," Johnson said and turned to walk away.

"I get off work about five," the secretary called after him. "Earlier if the jerk never returns."

"Thanks for the information," Johnson said, "but I'm going to be busy."

He found a telephone booth with directories still present in their holders. The yellow pages, though, looked as if they had been attacked by gypsy moths. Listings for computer firms, computer repairs, computer retail stores, and computer service were intact, however, and with a quick glance to both sides Johnson ripped those pages free. He settled on a park bench behind the public library to study them. Some he marked out immediately: computer repairs and computer service. Computer retail stores he studied a bit longer and then marked a few; he marked more of the computer firms. Afterward he pulled from his pocket a small photograph and looked at it speculatively before he went back to the lists and crossed out a few more addresses.

Finally he stood up and walked purposefully along the Avenue of the Americas for a few blocks, staring into windows filled with keyboards and display screens, frequently passing by with only a glance, sometimes venturing into the store and looking around quickly before leaving, once in a while asking a question of the clerk on duty. He returned toward Forty-second Street on Fifth Avenue, occasionally stepping into the lobbies of office buildings to scan their directories before returning to the street. He made a similar fruitless search up Madison Avenue and started back on Park. It was there, in the lobby of a tall office building, gleaming with freshly mopped marble and polished stainless steel, that he stood for a long time, staring at the directory, looking at the picture, and finally finding a spot near a newsstand where he could buy a newspaper and stand reading it unobtrusively while he watched the bank of elevators that served the top ten floors. A radio at the newsstand nearby was tuned to an all-news station that kept broadcasting hysterical bulletins, but occasionally, as if for change of pace, a cleverly worded human-interest item from a socialist country was inserted into the sequence of prewar news. The first time it happened, Johnson heard the vendor mutter angrily, the second time he said, "Would you listen to that?" and the third time, "Well, what do you know about that."

The elevators kept opening and shutting down the line that Johnson was watching. Sometimes people got on, but often they left empty. Sometimes people got off, but often the doors opened to an empty car and closed on emptiness as it answered a distant summons. There was something eerie about it, as if haunted by contemporary ghosts. Finally, after an hour, just before noon, the process speeded up, like a silent Hollywood comedy. Everybody was coming down. In the midst of one group Johnson spotted a short young man with a clean-shaven face and close-cropped red hair. He didn't look more than eighteen.

Johnson followed him through the revolving door onto the sidewalk and caught up with him halfway down the block. "Tom Logan?"

Logan gave him a quick, sidelong look as if he were accustomed to sizing up people in a single wary glance. He frowned. "You're not police," he said, but there was apprehension in his voice. "I've been staying clean."

"I'm not police."

"I don't want to go back," Logan said.

"I understand. I'm a private citizen. I need your help."

"I've got only an hour for lunch. You know, I've got to be punctual. I won't do anything dishonest. I'm through with that."

They were walking side by side. Johnson had fallen into Logan's hushed, sidelong way of speaking that no one near could overhear. "Why did they let you work for a computer firm?"

"You mean after I transferred ten million dollars to my own account?" Logan made a right turn toward Lexington. "They never caught on to that. It was when I started investing in old masters, and even that wouldn't have raised suspicion. I was paying for them out of secret Luxembourg accounts. No, it was when I had to go see them. It wasn't the computers that did it; it was the human element. Now, well, what better job for me than to train them to detect computer crime? Even the cops call me when they come across something suspicious."

They had reached a small, dingy Italian restaurant on Lexington, and Logan led the way into the dark interior, his shoulders twitching as if he wished Johnson would walk on past the entrance or disappear. But Johnson still was behind him when Logan stopped at a table with a red-checkered tablecloth and sat down. He sighed. "Okay, who are you, and what's your problem?"

"My name is Bill Johnson," Johnson said patiently, gripping the edge of the table with both hands as if to demonstrate that he was without guile or subterfuge, "and I want to stop the war that is going to happen in a few days now if we don't do something about it."

"We?" Logan echoed.

"You, me, everybody."

"Not me," Logan said. "I don't owe this world anything." He brushed away the waiter who appeared with water glasses and menus.

"How about ten million dollars?"

Logan shrugged. "That was just numbers in a computer."

"You've got more to lose than most people," Johnson said. "You're younger than most. You have a lot of living left."

"I've already done a lot of living, and most of it I didn't like. Besides," he said skeptically, "how could we stop a war?"

Johnson leaned forward and put his right elbow on the table to gesture with his right hand. "You and I can't, not all alone. And me—I'm helpless without you. But you and me and a bunch of others . . . ?"

"Get together?" Logan scoffed. "Get up and say, 'Stop this bad thing you're doing!' like the ban-the-bombers?"

"Nothing like that."

"Like what, then?" The waiter returned, but Logan gestured impatiently for him to go away when the man was still two tables away.

"If you had the right equipment, could you tap into the Pentagon computers?"

"You're talking espionage!" Logan said, jerking back. "Maybe treason!"

"Isn't there a difference between war secrets and peace secrets?" Johnson asked.

"Not to them guys. They're all secrets." Logan shivered.

"How about the Soviet military computer, the big one in Moscow?"

"Wait a minute! I haven't answered about the Pentagon yet!"

"You haven't said you couldn't."

"There isn't a computer anywhere I couldn't sneak into given enough time and good equipment, and the equipment doesn't have to be that good. But I haven't said I'd do it. This could get us killed."

"No one ever caught on to your financial manipulations. Besides, if we don't do it we're going to be killed anyway."

"There's that," Logan admitted. "But how do I know your plan has a chance?"

"How do you know it hasn't? You have to trust me. I could explain it, but we don't have the time. In any case, wouldn't it be better than simply waiting for the world to explode?"

"Maybe," Logan said. He had looked at his watch when Johnson had mentioned time. His watch was a complicated computer model. "I've got to go."

"You haven't had lunch."

"I've lost my appetite."

"Will you help?"

Logan hesitated. "Meet me at five. Where you picked me up when I stepped off the elevator. By the way, how did you know where— Oh, never mind! I'll tell you then."

CRISIS!

Johnson watched Logan's narrow shoulders until they passed through the door. They didn't seem to be twitching any more.

When Logan emerged from the elevator, his face was calm and confident. It was totally different from the look of scared cynicism he had turned to Johnson at noon. Now he looked no older than fifteen. "Okay," he said as Johnson moved up beside him, "when do we start?"

"Now."

"Good. But let's pick up some sandwiches. I'm starved. Where are we gonna do it?"

They were on the street now. A few people, having emerged from the building, were looking up at the sky as if seeing an ICBM would help them. New threats had been hurled as if they blazed trails in the sky for missiles to follow.

"Not here?" Johnson asked, waving his hand at the skyscraper behind them.

"Everything is sewed up tight," Logan said, looking up as if he could see the seams from here. "I showed them how. Maybe I could open things up again, but they've got heat sensors after hours, and they won't let me have a home computer. Conditions of parole."

"I have an idea," Johnson said.

With a sack of sandwiches and a carton of coffee, they walked into the Associated Press Building. "Wait here!" Johnson said as they reached the reception area. The receptionist was gone and the pace of activity had slowed, though reporters were scattered at desks around the big news room, and Frances Miller was still at work in her office. She came back to the reception area with Johnson.

"I've got a spare office with a computer terminal, but I

don't know why I let you talk me into these things. Him?" she said.

"Computer experts mature early. Like mathematicians," Johnson said. He smiled at Logan. "Tom has been telling me that kids are born today with computer skills, the way they used to be born knowing how to fix automobiles."

She sighed. "Follow me," she said, and led them to an office not far from hers, and left them alone.

Logan settled behind the terminal like a concert pianist easing himself into position behind a concert grand. For the first time since Johnson had seen him, he looked comfortable. Logan stretched his fingers in front of him and then wriggled them as if loosening them for a performance.

"Will it do?" Johnson asked.

Logan let his fingers rest lightly on the keyboard and pressed the "on" switch with one little finger. "All terminals are basically alike. The important thing is what they're hooked into. This one has connections all over the world, including, in one way or another, every computer that isn't self-contained, that has telephone or microwave links with other computers. If any of them anywhere is tied into a public information network, they can be breached."

"Does that describe the Pentagon computer and its counterpart in Moscow?"

"It should. You can't have a computer of the size and complexity they have to be that doesn't have to communicate with other computers and somewhere along the line pick up information from outside the network. It's just a matter of figuring out the weak points, the access keys, and the information codes."

"How long will that take?"

"Maybe a few hours. Maybe a few days."

"We haven't got a few days."

"I sure haven't," Logan said. "If I'm not back on the job at nine in the morning, I'd better be in the hospital or it's back in the slammer. Now, what is it I'm supposed to get out—or put in?"

"I'll tell you when I get back."

Johnson stuck his head into Frances Miller's office. "Come on," he said, "I'm going to take you to dinner."

"I've got too much to do," she protested, but the weariness that had begun to tug at her face and paint purple shadows beneath her eyes lifted for a moment.

"No excuses," Johnson said. He pulled her to her feet and marched her to the door. She went, laughing.

When they were outside, she asked more seriously, "How is it going?"

"The flames have receded a little," he said, "but they're still blazing in the background, waiting to return if we fail. Do you have a favorite restaurant?"

"There's a little French place that's open in the evening, just around the corner."

Over dinner she told him about her early life in Kansas City, her education at the University of Kansas, her experiences as a reporter on a series of newspapers, her marriage and its breakup, her first job with the Associated Press and the slow climb to her present position. . . . He listened attentively, interrupting only to ask questions at the right places.

"My second marriage was even shorter than my first," she said. "It is very difficult for a woman who has a satisfying career to achieve intimacy—" She broke off. "But you know all about that, don't you?"

But he had no stories to tell about himself.

When they returned to the office, Logan was sitting in

front of the computer terminal, staring at the screen intently as his fingers played across the keys, green lines of information marching across his face.

"We're back," Johnson said. Miller nodded and returned to her office.

Logan looked up reluctantly and smiled. "I haven't had this much fun since I ripped off the Chase Manhattan," he said. "I've got the Pentagon connection and a line on the Moscow computer. What do I do now?"

"What I want you to get for me is the U.S. diplomatic fallback position."

"What?"

"The final compromise we'd be willing to make to stop a nuclear war—if we got something in exchange from the Russians."

"And?"

"And feed it to the Russian computer in such a way that it looks accidental but calls attention to itself. As a last resort, put it on a cassette and we'll mail it to the Soviet embassy."

"What good will that do?"

"What you don't know you can't testify about if anything should go wrong—don't worry, nothing will go wrong. Then I want you to get the same information from the Russian computer—the ultimate compromise they'd be willing to make to keep the missiles from going off—and plant it in the Pentagon computer."

"What if I leave evidence?"

"Good," Johnson said. "It will help if they know their ultimate compromises have been compromised. We don't want to leave them thinking they know the secrets of the enemy and the enemy doesn't know theirs. They'll think they can take advantage."

"I get it," Logan said, his expression brightening and then darkening almost immediately. "I think."

"It doesn't matter, if you can get it done." When Logan turned back to the screen, Johnson stood for a moment with his forehead clasped in his right hand, leaning against the door frame.

At fifteen minutes past midnight, Logan, flushed and pleased, emerged from the office with two cassettes in his hand. "This one," he said, handing Johnson a cassette with a green label, "contains the Russian material. And this one"—he handed over a cassette with a red label—"contains the U.S. position. I guess I got the colors mixed up," he said apologetically.

"I'll remember," Johnson said. "Are you all done?"

"Complete. Wiped clean. Just a couple of false trails that suggest an accidental transfer of information to the enemy."

"That's great," Johnson said. "People feel better about bad luck than about espionage. Nevertheless, we can't trust them to discover the exchange on their own. I'll mail these in the morning. Tom, you've done a marvelous job. I don't think there's anyone else in the world who could have done it."

"I ought to thank you—I don't even know your name."

"Bill Johnson."

"Mr. Johnson. This was an opportunity to really have fun—and sort of make up for the kind of selfish use I made before of what I can do." He walked toward the elevators, his hands in his pockets, whistling, like Huck Finn heading for the frontier.

Johnson turned to follow him and saw Miller standing in the shadows. "Is that it?" she asked.

He nodded.

"Not the end of the world but the end of the war?"

"Hope for the future," Johnson said. "In my head the explosions are stopping one by one. The flames are dying down. The screams and shrieks are fading away. When I get these mailed off, maybe I can rest again."

"Won't there always be a new crisis?"

"Maybe I'll run out of them." But he smiled ruefully as if in recognition that he would never run out of them, not as long as there were people.

"Can I come with you? Back to the hotel?"

"Why would you want to?"

"You're more lonely—more alone—than any man I've ever met. And . . . I'm alone, too. Maybe, for a moment, we might not feel so isolated." She waited as if for a gift she did not deserve but wanted just as much.

"I might not know who you are in the morning," he said.

She smiled. "Oh, I think you will."

In the night she spoke his name. "Bill," she said. "Are you awake?"

"Yes."

"In case you do forget, I want to tell you now that if everything works out you have done something greater than—well, there's nothing to compare it with, except maybe the creation of the world."

"I didn't do anything—just gave people the opportunity to make the right decisions."

"Like me? Was that what I did?"

"Great events are propelled by great forces. Equal forces usually hold them back, but when those forces slacken and events get rolling toward some cataclysmic conclusion their momentum builds."

"Like news that reinforces people's beliefs in the inhumanity of the enemy?"

"Almost as if we can't work ourselves up to destroying an enemy unless we first convince ourselves that he isn't human. That's why we have to call them 'gooks' or 'fascists' or 'commies.' "

"And the stories I was distributing that described the enemy's humorous, sentimental, good-hearted moments—they made us pause and think. But what about Tom Logan? What did he do?"

"He gave the leaders on both sides a chance to save face—the opportunity to make concessions that the enemy knows you are willing to make, and in the assurance that the enemy also will make concessions that you know about in advance."

"What kind of concessions?"

"I don't know. Maybe you'll find out in the next few days, maybe not. I won't. I'll have forgotten. I was making a bad joke about forgetting you in the morning. That won't happen until I mail off the tapes. But the next morning. . . ."

The darkness in which their voices had hung disembodied was undisturbed for a moment. Then a voice said, "Bill?"

"Yes?"

"Maybe you should have something more to forget."

That was the end of the third day.

When he awoke in the morning she was gone. He looked around the room. It was not different in any meaningful way from the room in which he had awakened three days before: standard hotel. But there was one change. She had left something on the desk, a small machine.

He got up and walked slowly to it. The machine was a small cassette recorder. On it was a note, written not too legibly by a hand that had scribbled too many notes in a reporter's pad. It said, "Maybe this will help you remember."

He pushed the button marked "Play."

Her voice began. "This is Frances Miller, and I want you to remember the person who helped you when you needed help, and you helped more than you can know. . . ." There was more, but he stopped it. She thought it would be simple, but she didn't know what it was to have a mind like a slate periodically wiped clean. Tomorrow she would be a stranger, and he, a man who had no memory of her or their intimacies. No normal person could stand that. And he—he was weak. He did not dare allow himself a reason for not intervening.

He pressed the rewind button and began to record over the previous message. "Your name is Bill Johnson. You have just saved the world from World War III, and you don't remember. You will find stories in the newspaper about the crisis through which the world has passed. But you will find no mention of the part you played.

"For this there are several possible explanations. . . ."

Episode Two
Child of the Sun

He opened his eyes. He was lying on a bed. The sheets and blankets were tangled as if he had been thrashing around in his sleep.

He looked up at the ceiling. Cracks ran across the old plaster like a map of a country he did not recognize. On his left a window let a thin, wintry light through layers of dust. On the right was the rest of the room: shabby, dingy, ordinary. In the center of the room was a black-and-white breakfast table made of metal and plastic; pulled up to it were two matching metal chairs. Beyond the table, toward what appeared to be the door to the room, was a black plastic sofa; a rickety wooden coffee table stood in front of it, and a floor lamp, at one end. Against the left wall was a wooden dresser whose walnut veneer was peeling and, beside it, an imitation-walnut wardrobe. Against the right wall was another door which led, no doubt, to a bathroom. Next to the door four-foot partitions separated from the rest of the room a stove, a sink, a refrigerator, and cabinets.

Newspapers advertised it as a studio apartment; once it was called a kitchenette.

The man swung his legs out of bed and sat up, rubbing the sleep out of his face with open hands. He appeared to be a young man, a good-looking man with brown, curly hair and dark eyes and a complexion that looked as if he had been out in the sun. He had a youthful innocence about him, a kind of newly born awareness and childlike interest in everything that made people want to talk to him, to tell him personal problems, secrets they might have shared with no one else.

But after meeting him what people remembered most were his eyes. They seemed older than the rest of him. They looked at people and at things steadily, as if they were trying to understand, as if they were trying to make sense out of what they saw, as if they saw things other people could not see, as if they had seen too much. Or perhaps they were only the eyes of a man who often forgot and was trying to remember. They looked like that now as they surveyed the room and finally returned to the table and the hand-sized tape recorder that rested on it.

He stood up and walked to the table and looked down at the recorder. A cassette was in place. He pushed the lever marked "Play." The cassette hissed for a moment and then a man spoke in a clear, musical voice but with a slight accent, like someone who learned English after adolescence and speaks it better than the natives.

"Your name is Bill Johnson," the voice said. "You have just saved the world from World War III, and you don't remember. You will find stories in the newspapers about the crisis through which the world has passed. But you will find no mention of the part you played.

"For this there are several possible explanations, including the likelihood that I may be lying or deceived or insane. But the explanation on which you must act is that I have told you the truth: you are a man who was born in a future that has almost used up all hope; you were sent to this time and place to alter the events that created the future.

"Am I telling the truth? The only evidence you have is your apparently unique ability to foresee consequences—it comes like a vision, not of the future because the future can be changed, but of what will happen if events take their natural course, if someone does not act, if you do not intervene.

"But each time you intervene, no matter how subtly, you change the future from which you came. You exist in this time and outside of time and in the future, and so each change makes you forget.

"I recorded this message last night to tell you what I know, just as I learned about myself a few weeks ago by listening to a recording like this one, for I am you and we are one, and we have done this many times before. . . ."

After the voice stopped, the man called Bill Johnson picked up a billfold lying beside the recorder; near it were a few coins, a couple of keys on a ring, and a black pocket comb. In the billfold he found thirty-six dollars, a Visa charge card and a plastic-encased social security card both made out to Bill Johnson, and a receipt for an insured package dated three weeks before.

He tossed the billfold back to the table, walked to the stove, ran a little water from the hot water tap into a teakettle, and put it on the stove. He turned on the gas under it and tried to light it several times before he gave up and turned the knob off. He went into the bathroom, came out a few minutes later, and opened the front door. A newspaper lay on the dusty carpet outside. He picked it up, shut the door, and turned on the overhead light. The bulb burned dimly, as if the current was weak. He made himself a cup of instant coffee with tap water and took it to the table.

The newspaper was thin, only eight pages. The man leafed through it quickly before he stopped at one item, stared at it for a long moment as if he were not so much reading it as looking through it, tore it out, folded it, and put it into the billfold. He stood up, went to the dresser, put on his clothes, removed a scratched plastic suitcase from the top of the wardrobe, and put into it two extra pairs of pants, three shirts and a jacket, and a handful of socks and underwear; he put his dirty clothes into a paper sack and packed it, remembered the tape recorder, closed the suitcase, picked up the assorted objects on the table and slipped them into his pockets, and walked to the door.

He looked back. The room had been ordinary before. Now it was anonymous. A series of nonentities had lived here, leaving no impression of themselves upon their surroundings. Time itself in its passage had left a cigarette burn on the table, torn a hole in the cushion of a chair, ripped the sofa, scratched the coffee tables and the walls and the doors a thousand times, deposited loesses of dirt and lint in the corners and under the bed.

Johnson smiled briefly and shut the door behind him.

Downstairs he stooped to drop the keys on the ring into the mail slot in the door marked with a plaque on which was spelled out the word "Manager." Just after the keys hit the floor, the door opened. Johnson found himself looking into the face of a middle-aged woman. Her gray hair was braided and wound around her head; her face was creased into a frown of concern.

"Mr. Johnson," she said. "You're leaving? So sudden?"

"I told you I might." His voice was the voice he had heard from the tape recorder.

"I know. But . . ." She hesitated. "I thought—maybe—you were so good to my daughter when she had. . . her trouble. . . ."

"Anyone would have wanted to help," he said.

"I know but—she thought—we thought . . ."

Johnson spread his hands helplessly, as if he saw time passing and was unable to stop it. "I'm sorry. I have to leave."

"You've been a good tenant," the woman said. "No complaining about the brownouts, which nobody can help God knows, or the gas shortages. You're quiet. You don't take girls to your room. And you're easy to talk to. Mr. Johnson, I hate to see you go. Who will I talk to?"

"There are always people to talk to if you give them a chance. Good-bye," he said. "May the future be kind."

Only when Bill Johnson was alone did he feel like a person. When he was with people he felt that he was being watched. Those occasions had a peculiar quality of unreality, as if he were an actor mouthing lines that someone else had written for him and he was forced to stand off and watch himself perform.

Seeing himself at the corner of the block, windswept paper and dust swirling around his legs, waiting without impatience for a city bus to come steaming around the corner. Sitting uneasily over torn plastic protecting the seat of the pants from the sneaky probe of a broken spring, arriving at last at the interstate bus terminal surrounded by buildings with plyboarded windows scribbled with obscene comments and directions. Purchasing, with the aid of his credit card, a ticket automatically imprinted with a Las Vegas destination; waiting in a television-equipped chair—the viewer long broken and useless—until a faulty public-address system announced the departure of his bus in words blurred almost beyond understanding.

Hearing the unending whine of tires on interstate concrete, broken only by chuckhole thumps and the stepdown of gears as the bus pulled off the highway for one of its frequent stops to expel or ingest passengers, to refuel with liquefied coal and resupply with boiler water, to allow passengers to consume lukewarm food at dirty bus stations or anonymous diners. Enduring the procession of drowsy days and sleepless nights. Watching people enter and depart, getting on, getting off, individual worlds of perceptions and relationships curiously intersecting in this other world on wheels careening down the naked edges of the world.

Feeling bodies deposited in the seat beside him, bodies that sometimes remained silent, unanimated lumps of flesh, but sometimes, by a miracle as marvelous as the changing of Pinocchio into a real boy or the mermaid into a woman, transforming themselves into feeling, suffering, rejoicing, talking people.

Listening to the talk, this imperfect mechanism of communication, supplemented in the light by gesture and expression and body position, anonymous in the night but perhaps thereby as honest as the confessional.

Listening to an old man, hair bleached and thinned by the years, face carved by life into uniqueness, recalling the past as the present rolled past the window carrying him to the future, a retirement home where he never again would trouble his children or his grandchildren.

Listening to a girl, with blonde hair and blue eyes and a smooth, unformed face ready for the hand of time to write upon, anticipating rosily her first job, her first apartment, her first big city, her life to come with its romances, pleasures, possessions, and faceless lovers.

Listening to a man of middle years, dark-haired, dark-eyed, already shaped by a knowledge of what life was about and how a man went about facing up to it, touched now by failure and uncertainty, heading toward a new position, determined to make good but disturbed by the possibility of failing again.

Listening to a woman of thirty, her life solidified by marriage and family but somehow incomplete and unsatisfying, achieving neither the heights of bliss nor the bedrock of fulfillment, unconsciously missing the excitements of youth, the uncertainty of what the day would bring, the possibilities of flight and pursuit, looking, although she did not know it, for adventure.

The young man inspected the unrolling fabric of their lives and past it to that part yet concealed from them, and he was kind, as everyone must be kind who knows that the future holds bereavement, disappointment, disillusion, and death.

Besides, the times were hard: like the curse of the witch who had not been invited to the christening, the Depression had lain like death across the land for five years, the unemployment rate was nearly eighteen percent, and the energy shortage was pressing continually harder on the arteries of civilization. A little kindness came cheap enough, but it was scarce all the same.

Between conversations on his rolling world, the man

named Bill Johnson occasionally removed a newspaper clipping from his billfold and read it again.

CALIFORNIA GIRL ABDUCTED

Death Valley, CA (AP)—The four-year-old daughter of Ellen McCleary, managing engineer of the Death Valley Solar Power Project, was reported missing today.

McCleary returned from her afternoon duties at the Project to discover her housekeeper, Mrs. Fred Ross, bound and gagged behind her own bed and the McCleary girl, Shelly, gone from the home.

Authorities at the Project and the local sheriff's office have refused to release any information about the possible abductor, but sources close to the Project suggest that oil interests have reason to desire the failure of the Project.

McCleary was recently divorced from her husband of ten years, Stephen Webster. Webster's location is unknown.

Authorities will neither confirm nor deny that the abductor left a message behind.

Below the hill the valley was a lake of flame as Bill Johnson climbed toward the cottage some two hundred yards from the little group of preformed buildings he had left behind. Then, as the path rose, the angle of vision changed and the flame vanished, as if snuffed by a giant finger. Now the valley was lined with thousands of mirrors reflecting the orange-red rays of the dying sun toward a black cylinder towering in their center.

The air coming up the hill off the desert was hot, like a dragon's breath, and brought with it the scent of alkali dust and the feeling of fluids being sucked through the skin until, if the process continued long enough, only the desiccated husk would be left behind for the study of future archeologists. Johnson knocked on the door of the cottage. When there was no answer he knocked again, and turned to look at the valley, arid and lifeless below him like a vision of the future.

A small noise and an outpouring of cool air made him turn. In front of him, in the doorway, stood a middle-aged woman with a face as dry as an alkali flat.

"Mrs. Ross?" Johnson said. "I'm Bill Johnson. I talked on the telephone to Ms. McCleary from Las Vegas, but the connection was bad."

"Ms. McCleary gets lotsa calls," the woman said in a voice like dust. "She don't see nobody."

"I know that," Johnson said. He smiled understandingly. "But she will want to see me. I've come to help in the disappearance of her daughter."

Mrs. Ross was unmoved. "Lotsa nuts bother Ms. McCleary about stuff like that. She don't see nobody."

"I'm sorry to be persistent," Johnson said, and his smile illustrated his regret, "but it is important." His body position was relaxed and reassuring.

The housekeeper looked at him for the first time and hesitated about closing the door. As she hesitated, a woman's voice came from within the darkened house, "Who is it, Mrs. Ross?"

"Just another crank, Ms. McCleary," the housekeeper said, looking behind her, but grasping the door firmly as if in fear that Johnson would burst past her into the sanctity of the cool interior.

Another woman appeared in the doorway. She was tall, slender, dark, good-looking but a bit haggard with concern and sleeplessness. She stared at Johnson angrily as if she blamed him for the events of the past few days. "What do you want?"

"My name is Bill Johnson," he said patiently. "I called you from Las Vegas."

"And I said I didn't want to see you," McCleary said and started to turn away. "Shut the door, Mrs. Ross—" she began.

"I may be the only person who can get your daughter back for you," Johnson said. It was as if he had leaned a hand against the door to keep it from closing.

The tall woman turned toward him again, her body rigid with the effort to control the anxiety within. Johnson smiled confidently but without arrogance, looking not at all like a nut or a crank or a criminal.

"What do you know about my daughter?" McCleary demanded. Then she took a deep breath and turned to Mrs. Ross. "Oh, let him in. He seems harmless enough."

"The sheriff said not to talk to anybody," the housekeeper said. "The sheriff said you was to—"

"I know what the sheriff said, Mrs. Ross," McCleary interrupted. "But I guess it won't matter if I talk to this person. Sometimes," she continued, her voice detached and distant, "I have to talk to somebody." She brought herself back to this place and time. "Let him in and go stand by the telephone in case I find it necessary to call the sheriff." She looked at Johnson as if warning him against making that step necessary.

"I wouldn't want you to do that," he said submissively, and moved forward into darkness. More by sound than sight he followed her footsteps down a hallway into a living room where returning vision and the light filtering through closed drapes over a picture window let him make his way to an upholstered chair. McCleary sat stiffly on the edge of a matching sofa; it was covered in velvet with variable-width stripes of orange and brown and cream. She lit a cigarette. The lingering odors of stale smoke and a littered ashtray on the glass-covered coffee table in front of her suggested that she had been smoking one cigarette after another.

"What do you know about my daughter?" she asked. She was under control now.

"First of all," he said, "she is an important person." He held up a hand to forestall her questions. "Not just to you, overriding as that may be at the moment. Not just because she is a person in a society that values every individual. But because of her potential."

"What do you know about that?" she demanded. A note of doubt had crept into her voice.

"It's hard to explain without making me seem like a crackpot or a fool," Johnson said, leaning toward her to emphasize his sincerity. "I have—special knowledge—which comes to me in the form of—visions."

"I see." Doubt had crystallized into certainty. "You're a psychic."

"No," Johnson said. "I told you it was difficult. But if that's the way you want to think of it—"

"I've had dozens of letters and telephone calls from psychics since my daughter was abducted, Mr. Johnson, and they've all been phonies," she said coldly. "All psychics are phonies. I think you'd better go." She stood up.

He stood up along with her, not submitting to, but resisting his dismissal. He looked into her eyes as if his eyes had the power to compel her belief. "I think I can find your daughter. I think I know how to get her back. If

I thought you could do it without my help, I wouldn't be here. I want you to know that I could find myself in great difficulties and my mission in jeopardy."

"Where is my daughter?" It was not the tone of belief but of a final examination.

"With your husband."

"You guessed."

"No."

"You know about the message."

"Was there a message?"

"You're from Steve. He sent you."

"No. But I sense danger to your daughter and perhaps to your husband as well."

She slumped back to the sofa. "What are you then?" she asked. "Are you just a confidence man?" Her tone was pleading, as if it would comfort her if he admitted her guess was right. "What do you want from me? Why don't you leave me alone?" If she had been a more dependent person she might have turned her face from his and cried.

"All I want is to help you," he said, sitting down again, reaching toward her with one hand but not touching her, "and to help you find your daughter."

"I don't have any money," she said. "I can't pay you. If you're preying on my helplessness, it won't gain you anything. If you're seeking notoriety, you will be exposed eventually."

"None of these things matter beside your daughter's safety and her future. Moreover, you may not be able to control the events of your life as you have been accustomed to doing, but you are not helpless. I don't want any money. I don't want any word of my part in this to get out to anyone, and certainly not to the press. It would be dangerous to me."

"Then what do you want?"

"I want to get to know you," he said, and as she stiffened he hastened on, "so that I can find your daughter." His glance moved around the room as if he were looking at it for the first and the last time. At the picture window that looked out over the desert valley and the solar power project when the drapes were drawn. Michelle had stood there and watched for her mother's return. At the electronic organ in the corner that neither McCleary nor her daughter could play. At the doors that led to bedrooms where a woman and a man had slept and made love and lain awake in the night. At other doors that led to baths, to the hall, to the kitchen and dining room on the other side of the hall. "I want information about your work, your daughter, your husband, the circumstances of your daughter's abduction. . . ."

She sighed. "Where do you want to start?"

"The message. What did it say?"

"The sheriff told me not to describe it to anyone. He said that knowledge of it would either be guilty knowledge or proof of the abductor's identity."

"You've got to trust somebody some time," Johnson said.

"And the police are not to be trusted, Mr. Johnson?" Through her concern flashed the perceptiveness that had made her director of a major research project.

"From the police you get police-type answers," he said. "Investigation, surveillance, evidence, apprehension. I think you want something else—your daughter back safely and preferably without your husband—"

"My former husband," she corrected.

"Your former husband's injury or punishment."

"Ms. McCleary," said the voice of Mrs. Ross from the hall doorway, "the sheriff is here to see you."

"Thank you, Mrs. Ross," McCleary said.

"Come in, sir," Johnson said. "I've been expecting you."

The room was not much of a jail cell. It was a small room without windows. The walls were paneled in plywood faced with mahogany and decorated with framed prints of famous racehorses. In the center of the room was a long table lined with chairs on either side.

It had never been intended for a cell. It was a small dining room off the main cafeteria, where groups could get together for luncheon conversations. Now a young man sat across the table from Johnson, silent and nervous, uncertain about his duties and privileges as a jailer.

He was a junior engineer on the Solar Power Project, and he had been asked to guard the prisoner while the sheriff made arrangements to transport the prisoner to the county jail some forty miles away. The young man fidgeted in his chair, clasped and unclasped his hands, and smiled uncertainly at Johnson.

Johnson smiled back reassuringly. "How is the project going?" he asked.

"What do you mean?" The engineer was a pleasant-looking young man with sandy hair bleached almost white by the sun, a face peeling perpetually from sunburn, and large hairy hands that he didn't know what to do with.

"The Solar Power Project," Johnson said. "How's it going?"

"What do you know about the project?" the engineer demanded, as if he suspected that Johnson, after all, was the hireling of the oil interests.

"Everybody knows about the Solar Power Project," Johnson said. "It's no secret."

"I guess not," the engineer admitted. He looked at the metal table with its printed wood grain as if he wished it were a drawing board. "This is an experimental project, and we've demonstrated that we can get significant amounts of power out of solar energy."

"How much is that?"

"Enough for our own needs and enough more to justify the overhead towers that cross the hills toward Los Angeles," the engineer said with a mixture of pride and defensiveness.

"That is a significant amount."

"During daylight hours, of course."

"Then why is the project still experimental?" Johnson asked.

The young man at last found something to do with one hand. "Well," he said, rubbing his chin and making the day's stubble rasp under his fingers, "there's one problem we haven't solved."

"The daylight problem?"

"No. Energy can always be stored by pumping water, electrolyzing it into hydrogen and oxygen, with batteries or flywheels. The problem is economics: it's cheaper to burn coal, even if you toss in the cost of environmental controls and damage. Almost one-fourth as cheap. And nuclear power costs less than that. Other forms of solar power, including power cells for direct conversion of sunlight into electricity, are either less efficient or more expensive."

"If the project has accomplished its purpose," Johnson asked, "why is it still going on?"

Both the engineer's hands were in motion now as he

defended his project and his profession. "We still hope for a breakthrough. Producing cheaper solar cells through integrated factories. Maybe cheaper computer-driven mirrors. Maybe putting solar power plants in space where the sun shines twenty-four hours a day, if we could solve the problem of getting the energy back. Maybe some new method of converting sunlight into useful energy like chlorophyll or the purple dyes found in some primitive sea creatures."

"Nature's method of converting sunlight into energy may still be the most efficient," Johnson said. He looked up at one of the racehorses. It was a shiny red, and it was happily cropping blue grass inside a white rail fence.

"We're trying that, too," the engineer said. "Energy farms for growing trees or grasses. But put it all together and it doesn't add up to a third of the energy needs of the world that once were satisfied by cheap oil."

"What about nuclear energy?" Johnson asked.

"Inherently dangerous—particularly the breeder reactor. Not basically any more dangerous in its total impact than coal or oil, but the risks are concentrated and more visible. So the moratorium on the building of new nuclear power plants has effectively ended the effort to make nuclear energy safe."

"Well," Johnson said, "there's a lot of coal."

The engineer nodded. By now he was treating Johnson like an equal instead of a prisoner. "That's true," he said, "but unlike oil, coal is dirty. It has to be dug, and that damages the miners—or the land if it's strip-mined. Sulfur has to be removed, in one way or another, to avoid sulfur dioxide pollution. And the coal will run out, too, in a century or so."

Johnson looked sad. "Then the energy depression is

going to get worse until the coal runs out, and after that civilization goes back to the dark ages."

The engineer clasped his hands in front of him, almost in an attitude of prayer. "Unless we can come up with a workable technology for nuclear fusion."

"Fusing atoms of hydrogen together?"

"Making helium atoms and turning into energy the little bit of matter that's left over." The engineer's index fingers had formed a steeple. "The true sunpower—the solar process itself, clean, no radioactivity, inexhaustible, unlimited power without byproducts except heat, and maybe that could be harnessed to perform useful work if we're clever enough. Why, with hydrogen fusion man would have enough power to do anything he ever wanted to do—clean up the environment, raise enough food for everybody, improve living standards all around the world until everybody lives as well as we used to, return to space travel in a big way, reshape the other planets or move them into better orbits, go to the stars—" His voice stopped on a rising note like a preacher describing the pleasures of the life to come.

"But we haven't got it yet," Johnson said.

The engineer's eyes lowered to look at Johnson, and his hands folded themselves across each other. "We just haven't got the hang of it," he said. "There's a trick to it we haven't discovered, and we haven't got much time as civilizations go. For the past decade we've been through an energy depression that shows no signs of letting up. How much longer can we go on? Maybe thirty or forty years, if we're lucky and don't have a revolution or a major war; and if we don't discover the secret to thermonuclear fusion by then the level of civilization will be too low to apply the technology necessary to bring it into general use, and after that there'll be no one capable of thinking about anything except personal survival."

"Pretty grim," Johnson said.

"Ain't it?" the engineer said, and then he smiled. "That's why we keep working. Maybe we can buy a little time, ease the pressures a bit. Maybe somewhere a breakthrough will occur. If we don't find it, maybe our children will."

The engineer was a dreamer. Bill Johnson was a visionary. He knew what was coming, but the engineer jumped when the knock came at the door like the future announcing itself.

"George?" said the voice of Ellen McCleary. "Open up. I want to talk to the prisoner."

Outside the day had turned to night. The stars were out, bright and many-colored, and the Milky Way streamed across the sky like a jeweled veil. The reflected heat from the desert below seemed friendly now against the cool evening breeze pouring down from the hills.

Ellen McCleary stopped a few yards from the cafeteria building and turned to face Johnson. "I guess you think I'm a silly woman, not able to know her own mind, first having you arrested and then setting you free."

"I may think many things about you, but not that you're a silly woman," Johnson said. "That battle has been won; you don't have to keep fighting it. Your presence here as director of this project is proof of that."

"I thought about it," she said, shrugging off his interruption but not looking at him, "and I decided that I couldn't throw away the chance that you might be able to help. If I can get Shelly back—" She didn't finish the sentence. Instead she held out an oblong of stiff white paper. It was a Polaroid snapshot.

He took a few steps back into the light that streamed through the front window of the cafeteria building. The picture showed writing—red, broad, smeared—against a shiny black background.

"He wrote it on the bathroom mirror with my lipstick," she said.

Johnson read the message:

> *Ellen—The Court gave Shelly to you, but I'm going to give her what you never could—the full-time love of a full-time parent.*

"Is that your former husband's handwriting?" Johnson asked. He seemed to be looking through the picture rather than at it.

"Yes. His language, too. He's a madman, Mr. Johnson."

"In what way?"

"He—" She paused as if to gather together all the fugitive impressions of a life with another person. She took a deep breath and began again. "He thinks that the way he feels at the moment is the only thing that matters. That he may feel differently tomorrow or even the next moment doesn't count. He'd be willing to kill himself—or Shelly—if he felt like it at the moment." She let her breath sigh out. "That's what I'm afraid of, I guess."

"Are you sure he's homicidal?"

"I'm making him sound crazier than he is, I know, but what I'm trying to say is that he's an impulsive person who believes that people should only do what feels right to them. He doesn't believe in the past or the future. Now is the only thing that exists for him. He thinks I'm cold and unfeeling, and I see him as childish, and—but I'm talking as if you're a marriage counselor. We tried that, too."

They talked together now in the darkness, two voices without faces, sound without body. "That's all right," Johnson said. "It helps me get the feel of things. Did he have a profession, a talent, a job?"

Her voice held the hint of a shrug. "He was a bit of a lot of things—a bit of a painter, a bit of a writer, a bit of an actor, but a romantic all the time. What really broke things up, though, was when this project got started and I was selected as director. I was in charge, and he was just—around. He had nothing to do, and conditions were pretty primitive for a while. That's when Shelly was conceived—as sort of a sop to his manhood. But it didn't last. He left for a few months when Shelly was about a year old, came back, we quarreled, he left again, and finally I divorced him, got custody of Shelly, and that's about it."

"Not much for what—ten years of marriage?"

"Yes." She sighed. "Shelly is all, and he's taken her."

"Where did you meet?"

"In Los Angeles. At a party at a friend's house. I was a graduate student at Cal Tech; he was an actor. He seemed romantic and strong. I was—flattered, I guess—that he was interested in me. We got married in a whirlwind of emotion, and it was great for a few months. Then things began going bad. I irritated him by worrying about my career, by wanting to talk about where we were going to be next year, ten years from now. He annoyed me by his lack of concern for those things, by his unrelenting demands upon my time, my attention, my emotions. Part of my emotions were invested in other things—in my work, for one—and he could never understand that, or forgive it."

"I understand," Johnson said. "The times your husband left—did he return to Los Angeles?"

"I think he did the first time, although we weren't communicating too well then. But that's where he said he'd been when he came back."

"The second time?"

"I don't know. We didn't communicate at all until the divorce, and then it was through lawyers. Until that." She indicated the photograph in Johnson's hand, a shadowy finger almost touching the white rectangle.

He held it in his fingertips, almost as if he were weighing it. "I suppose the police checked all his friends in Los Angeles."

"And his relatives. That's where he was born and grew up. But they didn't find anything. Nobody has seen him recently. Nobody knows where he might have gone with Shelly."

"Did he have any hobbies?"

"Tennis. He liked tennis. And parties. And girls." The last word had an edge of bitterness.

"Hunting? Mountain climbing?" Johnson's words were tentative, as if he were testing a hypothesis.

She seemed to be shaking her head. "He didn't like the outdoors. Not raw. If he'd liked to hike or hunt, he still might be here," she said ruefully. The blur of a hand gestured at the mountains that rose to the east and the north and the west of them.

"He sounds restless," Johnson said. "Could he stay in one place for long at a time? If he starts moving around, the police will find him."

"He never has been able to stay still before, but if he

thought that was the only way to hurt me he might be able to do it."

"Is Mrs. Ross sure he's the one who tied her up?"

"She never knew Steve. I hired her after he left. But she identified his picture."

"There was nobody else with him? Nobody who might be making him do what he did?"

"Not that she could tell. She said he seemed cheerful. Whistled while he tied her up. Said not to worry, I would be back at six o'clock—that I was like a quartz watch, always right on the second. He hated that." She paused and waited in the darkness. When he didn't say anything, she asked, "Is there anything else?"

"Do you have any of his personal belongings?"

"I threw them out. I didn't want anything to remind me of him. Or to remind Shelly either, I guess. Except this." She handed Johnson another white oblong.

He took it into the light. It was the picture of a blond young man in tennis clothing, looking up into the sun with the net and court behind him, squinting a little, laughing, strikingly handsome and vital and alive, as if time had been captured and made to stand still for him and he would never grow old.

"Can I keep the pictures?" Johnson asked.

"Yes," she said. Her disembodied voice held a nod. "Can you find Shelly for me?"

"Yes," he said. It was not boastful nor a promise but a statement of fact. "Don't worry. I'll see that she gets back to you." That was a promise. "May the future be kind," he said. Then he walked out of the light into the darkness. His footsteps sounded more distant on the path until the night was still.

* * *

Los Angeles was a carnival of life, a sprawling, vivid city of contrasts between the rich and the poor, between the extravagant and the impecunious, between mansions and slums.

The smog was gone, removed not so much by the elimination of automobile exhaust fumes but by the elimination of the automobile. Except for the occasional antique gasoline-powered machines that rolled imperiously along the nearly deserted freeways, the principal method of transportation was the coal-fueled steam-powered bus. The smokestacks, too, had been stopped, either by smoke and fume scrubbers or by the Depression.

Watts was sullen. Unlike an earlier period when minorities had felt that they were being cheated of an affluence available to everyone else, the citizens shared what was clearly a widespread and apparently growing distress and general decline in civilization. The riots of discrimination were clearly past, and the riots of desperation had not yet begun.

Through this strange city went a man who did not know his name, troubled by a past he could not remember and visions of a future he could not forget, trying to put together a portrait of a man who had as many images as there were people who knew him, seeking the vision that would reveal a place where a man and a child might be unnoticed, asking questions and getting always the same replies.

At a Spanish bungalow with peeling pink stucco, "No, we don't know him."

At a walled studio with sagging gates, echoing sound stages, and decaying location sets that looked like a premonition of the society outside its walls, "No, we haven't used him in years."

At a comfortable ranch house in the valley, surrounded by orange trees, "The police have been here twice already. We've answered all their questions."

At a tennis club still maintaining standards and the muted *sprong-sprong* of court activity, "He hasn't been around for months."

At a high school where hopeless teachers tried to impart knowledge whose value they no longer found credible to listless students who were there only because society had no other place for them, "We can show you only the yearbooks," and in them pictures of a face without character and listings of activities without meaning.

And then, unexpectedly, at a bar along the Strip, half-facade and half-corrupt, like a painted whore, "Yeah, I seen him a couple of months ago, him and a fellow with a cap on—you know one of those things with a whatchmacallit on the front . . . yeah, a visor—like a sea captain, you know—yeah, Gregory Peck as Captain Ahab. Reason I remember—it wasn't his style, you know. It was always girls with him. You could see him turn up the charm like one of those things that dim and brighten lights . . . a rheostat?—yeah, I guess. With guys he was cool, you know?—like he didn't care what they thought of him. But with this guy it was different. Like he wanted something from the guy. . . . No. I didn't hear what they was talking about. I had sixty–seventy customers in here that night. The noise you wouldn't believe sometimes. You're lucky I remembered seeing him."

A search of the dock area, all up and down the coast, until finally at the small boat marina near Alamitos Beach State Park, a marina with many empty docks, "Steve? Sure, he borrowed my cruiser for a couple of hours about two weeks ago. . . . No, he didn't tell me where he was going, but I trusted him and he brought it back. Of course I didn't think he was running dope past the border. There's no point in that now, is there? What with the new laws and everything? Anyway, he was gone only a couple of hours. . . . Well, I gave him the keys about one o'clock in the afternoon, and he was back with them before four. . . . Sure I'm certain about the time. I remember—I told him I was having a party on board that evening, and I had to get her cleaned up and provisioned. Matter of fact, I asked if he wanted to join the party—a guy like Steve gives a party real class, and the girls come back—but he couldn't. . . . You can push her up to thirty knots, but she's a real fuel eater at that speed. . . . No, I didn't see anybody with him. May have been, but I didn't see anybody. Want to look at the boat? Why not? I bought it from a fellow in Long Beach five years ago when fuel got so expensive. Now I hardly ever go out in it. Use it sort of like a floating bar and bedroom. . . ."

Brass rails, gleaming teak decks, white paint shining in the sun, the spoked wheel, touch it, feel its response, sense the directions it has gone, the hands that have held it and steered the boat. The cabin below, all compact and efficient, bunks and tables, kitchen and head, immaculate, haunted by ghosts, crowded together here laughing, crying, drunken, reckless, desperate. . . .

And back to the dock, certain now, seeing a vision of a place available by water within an hour's range of the cruiser, at most thirty nautical miles from the small boat marina. . . .

And at the head of the dock, waiting for him, a tall, slender woman, dark-haired, dark-eyed, good-looking but a bit more haggard now. "So," she said, "he took her away by water. I would never have suspected him of having that much imagination."

Johnson looked at her and saw the past. "You didn't give him credit for much."

"You don't seem surprised at seeing me," she said.

"No."

She hesitated, looking down at her feet in their red canvas shoes that matched her red slacks. "I guess I owe you an apology," she said finally.

"No."

"I suspected you," she went on, looking up at him, letting him see her guilt. "The police suspected you too—of having had some contact with Steve, of being his emissary, at least of knowing him, perhaps where he was living, perhaps being willing to sell him out."

"You have reason to suspect people," Johnson said. The odor of fish and oily salt water surrounded them.

"So we had you followed. And you did the police work to find him. You don't know how difficult this is for me, do you?"

"Yes," he said.

"You did it better than the police. You found him. Maybe you really are what you say you are."

"That's a reasonable assumption."

"The world isn't reasonable," she complained. "People aren't reasonable. You did find him, didn't you? Tell me that you found him."

"I found him," Johnson said simply, "but I haven't gone to him yet. I haven't got Shelly back for you yet."

"I'm not asking you to tell me where he is," Ellen McCleary said, a bit unsteadily, looking at Johnson's face hopefully, "but I'm asking you to take me with you."

"I can get Shelly back without damage to her or your

former husband if I go alone," Johnson said. "With you along the chances get much slimmer."

She got angry at that. "Who are you to say? What do you know about him or me or Shelly? What right have you to meddle in our lives?"

"Only the outcome can justify any of us," he said. "Good intentions, emotional involvements, rights—all these are only the absolution we give ourselves for lack of foresight. Look out there." He motioned toward the smooth blue swells of the Pacific gleaming with highlights in the sunshine. "Quite a difference from your wasteland. That's fertility. That's promise. We came from the sea, and in the sea lies our future."

"My desert is not as lifeless as it looks," she said. "We get energy from it, energy we need, energy we must have."

"The lowest kind of energy—heat. You waste a lot when you have to pump it up into electricity."

"Like all energy it comes from the sun."

"Not all," he said. The wind was coming in off the ocean and blowing away the old smells of rot and waste. "I won't take you with me. You can have me followed, of course, but I ask you not to do that. What will it be? Your desert of old memories or my sea of hope?"

She shook her head slowly, helplessly. "I can't promise."

"Then neither can I," he said, and left her standing at the edge of the water as he walked quickly to the street and the nearest public transportation.

The ferry ride was a pleasant interlude, a break in the feeling of urgency that drove Johnson. He could not hurry the ship, and he existed for the moment, like the smiling young man in the tennis clothes, outside of time. From

San Pedro Bay to Santa Catalina, he watched the blue water curl under the bow, white and playful, and the smooth blue surface of the Pacific extending undisturbed to the end of the world.

Johnson studied it as if he had never before seen the protean sea or the creatures that lived in it—small darting fish, dark shapes changing instantly into silver when pursued by large solitary predators, and distantly, across the horizon, the gray unbelievable backs of whales. The breeze, laden with salt, blew across his face and tugged at his hair and clothing, and he smiled.

He left the ferry at Avalon as soon as the ship had tied up in its slip.

Few people got off the ferry—the pleasure business was an early casualty of the Depression—and Johnson paid no attention to them. He rented a bicycle from a stand at the end of the pier and pedaled up the main road among the wooded hills, got off and walked the bicycle where the hills were too steep to ride, stopped for a moment when he had reached the high point, with Black Jack Peak to his right and the Pacific spread out in front of him again like hope regained, then coasted rapidly down the hills, past Middle Ranch and along the west coast where the ocean flashed blue between the trees.

Just short of Catalina Harbor, he stopped, pulled the bicycle off the road and behind some trees, and walked up through the woods along a barely discernible path until the trees began to thin and he found himself close to a small clearing with a small cabin in the middle. As Johnson stood without moving, the sound of a child's happy voice came to him and then a man's deeper voice followed, surprisingly, by a third voice and a fourth, the child's squeal of laughter, and a man's chuckle.

Johnson moved through the last of the trees into the dust of the clearing. Now he could see the front porch of the cabin. On the edge of the porch sat a child with short dark hair and lively blue eyes. She was dressed in a red knitted shirt and dirty jeans. Her feet were bare, her hands were squeezed ecstatically between her knees, and she stared enraptured at finger puppets on the hands of a light-haired young man.

In a hoarse voice the young man chanted:

> "Today I'll brew, tomorrow bake;
> Merrily I'll dance and sing.
> Tomorrow will a baby bring:
> The lady cannot stop my game . . ."

The little girl shouted with delight, "Rumpelstiltskin is my name!"

The young man was laughing with her until he saw Johnson. He stopped laughing. The puppets fell off his fingers as he reached behind him. The little girl stopped laughing, too, and looked at Johnson. In repose her face looked a great deal like the face of Ellen McCleary with the young man's blue eyes and spontaneity.

"Hello," Johnson said. He moved forward slowly, like a man moving among wild animals, so as not to frighten them into flight or attack.

"Don't tell me you've come to read the meter," said the young man sitting on the porch, "or that you just wandered here by mistake."

Johnson eased himself down in the center of the clearing with his back to the ocean that gleamed through the trees a deeper blue than the sky. He sat cross-legged and helpless in the dust and said, "No, I came here to talk to you, Steve Webster."

Webster brought his right hand out from behind him. It had a revolver in it. He supported the butt on his knee and pointed it in Johnson's general direction. "If you're from my wife, tell her to leave me alone—me and Shelly—or she'll regret it." Webster's voice was harsh, and the little girl stirred nervously beside him, looking at her father's face, down at the gun, and then at Johnson.

"I've talked to your former wife," Johnson said, "but I'm not here in her behalf alone. I'm here as much for your sake as hers, but mostly for Shelly's sake."

"That's a lot of crap," Webster said, straightening the gun a little.

"You're frightening your daughter," Johnson said to him.

"She wasn't frightened before you came," Webster said.

"I realize that you and your daughter have been happy together," Johnson said. He spread his hands as if he were weighing sunbeams on his palms. "But how long can it last? How long before the authorities locate you?"

Webster waved the ugly gun in the air as if he had forgotten he held it. "That doesn't matter. Maybe they'll find us tomorrow, maybe never. Now we're happy. We're together. Whatever happens can never change that."

"Suppose," Johnson said, "it could last forever. You can't always be a little girl and her father playing games in a cabin in the woods. Shelly will grow up without schooling, without friends. Is that the thing to do for your daughter?"

"A man has got to do what he thinks is right," Webster said stubbornly. "Now is all any of us have got. Next month, next year, maybe something else will happen. Something good, something bad—you can't live for that. Nobody knows what's going to happen."

Johnson's lips tightened but Webster didn't seem to notice.

"Nobody's found me yet," Webster said, and then his eyes focused on Johnson again. "Except you." He noticed the gun in his hand and pointed it more purposefully at Johnson. "Except you," he repeated.

The little girl began to cry.

"Wouldn't that spoil it?" Johnson said. "Having Shelly see me shot by her father?"

"Yeah," Webster said. "Run inside the cabin, Shelly," he said, looking only at Johnson. The little girl didn't move. "Go on, now. Get in the cabin." The little girl cried harder. "See what you're making me do?" he complained to Johnson.

Johnson put his hands out in the dust in a gesture of helplessness. "I'm not a threat to you, and you can't save anything by getting rid of me. If I can find you, others can. In any case, you couldn't stay here long. You'll need food, clothing, books. Word about a man and a little girl living here is bound to get out. You'll have to move. The moment you move the police will spot you. It's hopeless, Steve."

Webster waved the gun in the air. "I can always choose another ending."

"For yourself? Ellen said you might do that."

"Yeah?" Webster looked interested. "Maybe for once Ellen was right."

"But that's not the way it ought to be," Johnson said. "You're old enough to make your own decisions, but you ought to leave Shelly out of this. She's got a right to live, a right to decide what she wants to do with her life."

"That's true," Webster admitted. He started to lower the gun to his knee again, and then lifted it to point at

Johnson again. "But what does a little girl know about life?"

"She'll get bigger and able to make her own decisions if you give her a chance," Johnson said.

"A chance," Webster repeated. He raised the gun until it pointed directly at Johnson, aiming it, tightening his finger on the trigger. "That's what the world never gave me. That's what Ellen never gave me."

Johnson sat in the dust, not moving, looking at the deadly black hole in the muzzle of the gun.

Gradually Webster's finger relaxed. He lowered the revolver to the porch beside him as if he had forgotten it. "But you're not to blame," he said.

"I suppose I'm to blame," a woman's voice said from the edge of the clearing. Ellen McCleary stepped out from among the trees.

Webster seemed surprised and delighted to see her. "Ellen," he said, "it was good of you to come to see me."

"Mommy," Shelly said. She tried to get up and run to her mother, but Webster held her wrist firmly in his hand and would not let her go.

"That's all right, Shelly," Ellen said, moving easily toward the porch where her former husband and her daughter sat. She no longer seemed tired, now that she had reached the end of her search. "Let Shelly go," she said to Webster.

"Not bloody likely," he said.

"Not to me," Ellen said. "Let her go with this man."

Webster glanced at Johnson. Neither of them said anything.

"Let's leave Shelly out of this," Ellen said. "It's between us, isn't it?"

"Maybe it is," Webster said. His fingers loosened on Shelly's wrist.

The little girl had stopped crying when her mother appeared. Now she looked back and forth between her parents, on the edge of tears but holding them back.

"We did it to each other," Ellen said, "let's not do it to Shelly. She's not guilty of anything."

"That's true," Webster said. "You and I—we're guilty, all right."

"Go to Mr. Johnson, Shelly," Ellen said. Her voice was quiet but it held a quality of command.

Webster's hand fell away, and he pushed the little girl affectionately toward Johnson. "Go on, Shelly," he said with rough tenderness. "That man's going to take you for a walk."

Johnson held out his arms to the little girl. She looked at her father and then at her mother, and turned to run to Johnson.

"That's a kind thing to do," Ellen said.

"Oh, I can be kind," Webster said. He grinned, and his face was warm and likeable.

Johnson got slowly to his knees in the dust of the clearing and then to his feet.

"It's a matter of knowing what kindness is," Webster said.

"If you're fixed in the present," Ellen said, "I suppose that would be a problem."

Johnson took Shelly's hand and began moving out of the clearing.

"Now, now," Webster cautioned, "let's not be unkind. We are put here on this earth to be kind to one another. And we have come together now to be kind to one another as we were not kind before."

Johnson and Shelly had reached the protection of the trees and moved among them. The odor of green growing things rose around them.

"The problem," Ellen said, "is that we don't know what the other one means by kindness. What is kindness to you may be unkindness to me, and the other way around."

As Johnson and Shelly moved down the path, they could hear the voices behind them.

"Don't start with me again," Webster said.

"I'm not," she said. "Believe me, I'm not. But it's all over, Steve. I didn't come here alone, you know."

"You mean you brought police," he said. His voice was rising.

"I couldn't find you by myself," she said. "But I didn't bring them. You brought them. By what you did. Don't make it worse, Steve. Give yourself up." The rest was indistinguishable. But the sound of voices, louder, shouting, came to them until hands reached out of bushes beside the path to grab them both.

A man's voice said, "You're not Webster."

Another man's voice, on the other side of the path, said, "That's all right, little girl, we're police officers."

A shot came from the clearing some two hundred yards away. For a moment the world seemed frozen—the leaves were still, the birds stopped singing, even the distant sea ceased its restless motion. And then everything burst into sound and activity again, bodies pounded past Johnson toward the clearing, dust hung in the air, and Shelly was crying.

"Where's my mommy?" she said. "Where's my daddy?"

Johnson held her tightly in his arms and tried to comfort

her, but there was nothing he could say that would not leave her poorer than she had been a few moments ago.

Then he heard footsteps approaching on the path.

"Hello, Shelly," Ellen said heavily.

"Mommy!" the little girl said, and Johnson let her go to her mother.

After a moment, Ellen said over the child's head, "You knew what was going to happen, didn't you?"

"Only if certain things happened."

"If I had not come here Steve might still be alive," she said, "and if you hadn't been here both Shelly and I might be dead."

"People do what they must—like active chemicals, participating in every reaction. Some persons serve their life purposes by striding purposefully toward their destinations; others, by flailing out wildly in all directions."

"What about you?"

"Others slide through life without being noticed and affect events through their presence rather than their actions," Johnson said. "I am—a catalyst. A substance that assists a reaction without participating in it."

"I don't know what you are," Ellen said. "But I've got a lot to thank you for."

"What are you going to do now?"

"I'm going to sit down and think for a long time. Maybe Steve was right. Maybe I was neglecting Shelly."

"Children can be smothered as well as neglected," Johnson said. "They must be loved enough to be let go by people who love themselves enough to do what they must do to be people."

"You think I should go back to my project."

"For Shelly's sake."

"And yours?"

"And everyone's. But that's just a guess."

"You're a strange man, Bill Johnson, and I should ask you questions, but I have the feeling that whatever answers you gave or didn't give, it wouldn't matter. So—let me ask you just one." She hesitated. "Will you come to see me again when all this is over. I—I'd like you to see me as something other than a suspicious, harried mother."

An expression like pain passed across Johnson's face and was gone. "I can't," he said.

"I understand."

"No, you don't," he said. "Just understand—I would like to know you better. But I can't."

And he stood on the hillside, dappled by the light that came through the leaves and was reflected up from the ocean, and he watched them walk down the path toward the road that would take them back to the boat, back to the mainland.

In the distance a frigate bird sailed alone in the sky, circling a spot in the ocean, turning and circling and finding nothing.

The rented room was lit only by the flickering of an old neon sign outside the window. Johnson sat at a wooden table, pressed down a key on the cassette recorder in front of him, and after a moment began to speak.

"Your name is Bill Johnson," he said. "You have just returned to her mother the little girl who will grow up to perfect the thermonuclear power generator, and you don't remember. You may find a small item in the newspaper about it, but you will find no mention of the part you played in recovering the girl.

"For this there are several possible explanations. . . ."

After he had finished, he sat silently for several minutes while the cassette continued to hiss, until he remembered to reach forward and press the lever marked "Stop."

Episode Three
Man of the Hour

The first thing he saw when he opened his eyes was the audio cassette dangling by a string from the remains of a metal light fixture surrounding a naked bulb in the ceiling. The bulb was dark but the room was partially illuminated by the sunlight streaming through rips in the blind that tried to shade the window to his right. One stray sunbeam fell across the old wrought-iron bed in which he was lying on his back, the white chenille bedspread with its pattern worn down to random tufts and a thin, pink cotton blanket bunched at the foot of the bed, and under him a mattress in which the springs had long since chosen anarchy.

The room was small, no more than twelve feet wide and fifteen feet long, and it was dirty in ways that no sweeping and scrubbing could eradicate. Dirt was ground into the pitted plastic of the floor and pounded into cracks in the walls and the ceiling. The room even smelled dirty, of ancient hamburgers and pizzas and tacos smuggled into the room in paper sacks and their crumbs and drips left where they had fallen, of the sweet and sweaty stink of poverty. And the room was hot. The window was half raised, and occasionally a gust of humid air would flap the shade and roll the dust kitties across the floor and rattle the heap of insect carcasses on the scarred wooden table under the light.

The man on the bed who did not know his name rolled onto his side and then sat up, his feet flat on the sticky floor. He was a pleasant-looking young man with curly brown hair and dark eyes and a well shaped but not heavily muscled body whose skin had a brown cast to it. He was about five feet ten, not tall enough nor short enough to be noticeable. Nothing about him was remarkable. His chest was hairless. He had been sleeping in his boxer shorts.

He stood up, testing his balance as if he had to think about it, wiggling his fingers, his arms extended, as if to check the messages his nerves sent up his arms to his brain, rotating his shoulders experimentally. He reached the table in the center of the floor with two short steps, and reached out for the dangling cassette. He pulled it free with one hand, breaking the string that held it to the ceiling fixture, and turned it over. Something was printed in neat small letters on the sticker attached to it. "IMPORTANT INFORMATION," it said.

The man looked around the room, at the two rung-backed wooden chairs next to the table, at the ruined upholstered chair in the corner with the old reading lamp on a flexible metal arm rising over the back like a frozen cobra, at the three battered wooden doors set into adjacent walls. One of them was narrower than the others and occupied a sill six inches off the floor. Behind it was a bathroom tiled in black and white plastic squares; nearly half the tiles were missing. When the man came out he put on the clothing he found hanging in a closet behind one of the doors. The clothing was neater and newer than the room: a light-blue dress shirt, a pair of gray slacks, a gray tweed jacket, a pair of brown shoes, relatively unscuffed, fairly recently shined. An old suitcase stood in the back of the closet.

On the table was a small heap of belongings: a few coins, a hotel key with the number "506" incised into it, a black pocket comb, and a billfold. In the billfold were three dollar bills, a pawnshop ticket, a Visa credit card, and a plastic-encased social security card. The credit card and the social security card carried the name "Bill Johnson." The credit card had a note attached to it with a paper clip. The note was printed on yellow, ruled paper and said, "This card is overdrawn. If you try to use it, you may be arrested." The man removed the note and put it into his jacket pocket along with the paper clip, put the cards into his billfold with the dollar bills, picked up the cassette and put it in the other pocket.

Behind the third door was a dim hallway lighted only by a gray window at the far end. A thin, dusty runner was tacked to the center of the wooden floor. Halfway down the hall the man came upon the dejected black metal doors of an elevator. When he pushed the button beside the doors, he heard no movement, no response, distant or near, and he turned and walked to a nearby stairwell. Five dark flights of stairs down, the staircase emerged into a dusty lobby. A few overstuffed chairs, in scarcely better shape than the one in the man's room, sagged in the corners. Between two of them was an oak library table from which the veneer was peeling in places. On it was an imitation Tiffany lamp. Beside the lamp was a torn envelope and an old *Time* magazine.

The man looked at the magazine as if he wanted to pick it up, but behind the desk to the left a thin, sour voice said, "Mr. Johnson. I hope you have the money to pay your overdue bill. Otherwise. . . ."

"I'll get it today," the man said. "Tomorrow at the latest. Is there a store near here where I can play a cassette?"

"If I were you," said the man behind the desk, who had risen to his feet and leaned bony elbows on the counter, "I'd worry about getting a job and not about no music."

"It will help me get a job."

The man behind the desk jerked his head toward his left shoulder. "Just down the street there's a music store," he said. "Least there was. Maybe they're still in business." His voice was skeptical but a bit less strident.

"Thanks," the man said.

"How come you don't say 'may the future be kind,' " the desk clerk asked in a tone that was almost friendly, "like you always do?"

"May the future be kind," the man said.

A hot merciless wind blew down the nearly deserted street carrying dust and bits of paper. No cars were parked along the curb, but here and there a stripped hulk appeared like the bones of a dinosaur unearthed from strata of garbage and old newspapers. No cars disturbed the potholed streets. Here and there solitary figures skulked along the boarded store- and building-fronts, but they no longer had the spirit to be dangerous. One approached the better-dressed man and held out its hand in ritual but hopeless appeal. He put a dollar in it. As if by magic, ragged children appeared with their hands out, and the man gave away his other dollar bills and the coins in his pocket before he demonstrated that his billfold and his pockets were empty and the beggars disappeared as quickly as they had assembled.

Like the rest of the world, the music store had seen better days. Actually it was a used music store, with long-playing records in battered cardboard envelopes racked in bins and cassettes, with and without plastic cases, tossed into heaps on tabletops. In the air was the lingering odor of an aromatic herb only slightly masked by the smell of incense. An aging young woman with long, black, uncombed hair stood behind a narrow counter toward the front of the dark shop. She wore a shapeless gown printed with blue and yellow flowers; it exposed one white shoulder. She swayed back and forth with her eyes half closed as if hearing some internal melody.

"May I listen to one of the cassettes?" the man asked after a moment of standing in front of the woman without being noticed.

With a slow wave of her right hand, the woman motioned toward a dingy, glassed-in booth at the back of the shop. The man made a pretense of sorting through the cassettes on the table near the counter and then picking one. In the glass booth he slipped the cassette from his pocket and placed it in an old machine that seemed fastened to the counter. When he clicked the cover down and pressed a lever marked "Play," a voice boomed out. Quickly he turned down the volume to where he could barely hear it.

". . . name is Bill Johnson," the cassette player said imperfectly. "You have just returned to her mother the little girl who will grow up to perfect the thermonuclear power generator, and you don't remember. You may find a small item in the newspaper about it, but you will find no mention of the part you played in recovering the girl.

"For this there are several possible explanations, including the likelihood that I may be lying or deceived or insane. But the explanation on which you must act is that I have told you the truth: you are a man who was born in a future that has almost used up all hope; you were sent to this time and place to alter the events that created that future.

"Am I telling the truth? The only evidence you have is your apparently unique ability to foresee consequences—it comes like a vision, not of the future because the future can be changed, but of what will happen if events take their natural course, if someone does not act, if you do not intervene.

"But each time you intervene, no matter how subtly, you change the future from which you came. You exist in this time and outside of time and in the future, and so each change makes you forget.

"I recorded this message last night to tell you what I know, before I had to pawn the recorder for money to make a partial payment on the room, just as I learned about myself a few days ago by listening to a recording like this one, for I am you and we are one, and we have done this many times before. . . ."

After the voice stopped the tape continued to hiss past the sound head while the man named Johnson stood in the dust-covered, glassed-in booth staring through the darkened store toward the glowing rectangles of the door and the front window. Then he shook his head as if to loosen the cobwebs inside it, stopped the player, retrieved the cassette, and slipped it into his pocket while he picked up

CRISIS! 89

the one he had placed beside the machine. He opened the door and walked toward the front of the store and put the cassette in his hand back onto the table.

"Sorry," he said, but the woman at the counter wasn't paying attention to anything but the music in her head. "Do you know where I might get a job?" he asked. The woman didn't respond. "Do you have any idea where a man might apply for a job?" Johnson asked again.

The woman waved her left hand. Johnson opened his mouth as if to ask again when he glanced in the direction the woman had waved. Across the street was a billboard in a vacant lot where a building had been torn down. On the billboard was the picture of a man with white hair but a youthful, tanned, strong face. The face was serious, concerned, sympathetic. Beside the face were the words: "Out of work? I'll hire you." And below that, in smaller letters: "Apply at: . . ." Then came an address in slightly different letters, as if the poster had been printed without them and the address inserted afterward. Under the picture was a name in letters as large as the message: "Arthur King."

Johnson looked at the billboard for a long time, much longer than necessary to read and understand the simple message. His eyes were open and slightly unfocused, as if he were not so much looking at the billboard as beyond it. Then he shook himself like a person trying to rid himself of unwanted thoughts. "Thanks," he said. He paused at the door and looked back at the woman. "May the future be kind."

She did not reply.

The employment office was in a distant part of the city that Johnson learned was Los Angeles, and it took him more than two hours to walk there. The office was located in a warehouse jury-rigged with portable plastic partitions and fluorescent light fixtures dangling from chains and cords, and cords snaking across the floor. The building was in a district with small factories and other warehouses, but here the atmosphere was different. The wind was still hot, but the streets had been swept, cars and trucks moved along them, the buildings were occupied, and people walked on the sidewalks as if they had a destination and a purpose. Above the warehouse and most of the other buildings was a sign that read: "King International."

After the street the warehouse was cool and dusky. In a few seconds Johnson's pupils expanded. A large bare room was filled with people. At first they seemed like an unorganized mob, and then order began to appear. They formed a line beginning at an open doorway in a wall forty feet from the entrance and serpentining its way to cover most of the space between the side walls that were almost twice as far apart as from front to back.

People came through the door behind Johnson and brushed past him to join the near end of the line before he, too, went to stand in it and was, in turn, followed by others who kept coming and coming until he was merely a part of a process. Uniformed men and women with the words "King International" embroidered within an oval on their left breast pocket kept it a human process, however. They moved among the waiting jobseekers with folding chairs, coffee, soft drinks, doughnuts, and words of encouragement. "Please be patient," they said sympathetically. "Don't worry. There are jobs for everybody. But it will take a little time."

Behind Johnson someone snorted. "A little time," a cultivated voice said scornfully. "It's taken five years."

Johnson turned. The man behind him was lean and

middle-aged. He had iron-gray hair and bushy eyebrows and a face that looked as if it had been carved from the side of a mountain, but as he noticed Johnson's gaze the stone turned into a sardonic smile. "Howdy, friend," he said in an imitation of midwestern neighborliness.

"I'm very well," Johnson said, "and how are you?"

The other man dropped his pretense when he heard Johnson's voice. "Better than I have been," he said. "There's been a lot of misery around, and I've had my share."

His name, he said, was Robert Scott, and he had been a professor of political science in the days when society could afford universities and people could afford to attend them. But he had been released—"terminated, in the language of the profession"—during the early days of the Depression, and ever since he had been unable to find work except for some editing and ghost-writing assignments that had dwindled into proofreading and then to nothing. "I worked my way through college as a television technician, but there hasn't been anything in that line either. King has its own communications section, however."

Johnson did not talk about himself. Instead he asked questions and brought the conversation back, finally, to Scott's original skepticism about the lengthy wait. "Surely if King advertises jobs for everyone, he will have to supply them."

"Sure he will," Scott said. "I'm not worried about that, even though it doesn't seem likely that even the biggest conglomerate in the world can afford to hire everyone that's out of work. But if it could, why did it wait so long?"

Johnson looked curious. Scott looked to either side as if he feared that he might be overheard and what he said might endanger his chances of employment. He lowered his voice. "I'll tell you why. Because King is one of the few companies that have prospered during the Depression."

"Surely that is an indication of good management," Johnson said.

"I'll give King credit for that," Scott said, "though I wonder about an enterprise that profits when everybody else is miserable. He's shrewd enough. Maybe too shrewd."

"How can his offer be anything but generous?"

The line shuffled forward. Scott looked around to see if any of the people in uniform were near. "King has bought up a lot of distressed industries recently, farms at bargain prices, and has negotiated a great many contracts that will be real moneymakers if the economy picks up and people start buying again."

"How do you know these things?"

"It's in the papers. You can put it together if you're looking. And just because I'm unemployed doesn't mean I can't read; the public library still is open a couple of hours a day."

"So what King pays people he will get right back when they buy the food and other goods he produces."

"They're going to spend everything they make, all right. And it's going right back into King's pocket. Plus the money from the people he doesn't pay. Plus the increase in prices as the economy improves. The contracts he owns will be worth two or three times as much as he paid for them. The industries he doesn't own will want to hire more people, but they will have to get them from him."

"But isn't he doing what government could have done—should have done? Put people back to work? End the Depression?"

"Government is unwieldy and pulled in dozens of directions by thousands of influences. And it's bound by laws and regulations, some of which King has persuaded Congress to waive, like the minimum wage."

"If Congress can waive it, Congress can reinstate it."

"They won't have to," Scott said. "King will raise wages himself before the cry goes up for him to do so."

"If government can't get the country out of a Depression, surely we should be grateful to someone who can. Even if he makes a profit at it."

"Grateful?" Scott said. "Sure. And if it's only profit King is after, I guess the world can survive that. It survived Henry Ford, who paid his workers five dollars a day during a Depression when the standard was less than half that, and they made him a billionaire. But I've got a feeling there's something else behind this, and I'm going to find out what it is."

But soon it was the end of the day, and they had nothing to show for their wait but a card attesting to their place in line.

By the middle of the second day Johnson and Scott were allowed to pass through the far door with a group of ten other applicants. They faced a corridor with a row of cubicles on either side of it and a man and woman in uniform passing out questionnaires and forms and pencils.

"So long, Johnson," Scott said. "Good luck. Keep in touch." He smiled ironically.

"That might not be so easy to do," Johnson said. "But I have a feeling we will meet again. And good luck to you. Whatever you do, don't give up."

"I won't," Scott said grimly. "I'll keep digging."

"I know you'll do that," Johnson said. "I mean on life

and people. Give them a chance and they'll come out the right way."

"I think you believe that. I hope you're right." But Scott shook his head as he accepted papers and pencil.

The cubicle was not much larger than a voting booth. It held a small table and a chair. Johnson sat down and filled out an employment questionnaire and a psychological evaluation form. It took him a while. At some of the questions he stared for several minutes before finally putting down an answer; others he simply left blank. By the time he was done Scott and all the others with whom he had been admitted were gone. The uniformed woman who took his papers told him to return the next day for an interview.

"I don't have any money," he told her, "and all I've had to eat in the past two days are the doughnuts and coffee you've passed out."

She smiled sympathetically and gave him a card. "Print your name here and sign it, and the cashier as you go out will advance you ten dollars against whatever salary you finally earn."

"What if I don't come back?"

She smiled again. "You'll be back. No one wants to miss out on a job. If by some strange chance you don't, King International will consider it charity. That's the way Mr. King wants it."

"Bless Mr. King," Johnson said without irony.

"That's what they all say."

The next morning Johnson was admitted to the presence of a weary interviewer. She had an office with real, though movable, walls made of plywood, a standard-size metal desk with a computer terminal, and two metal-and-plastic chairs. The interviewer was a dark-haired young woman in tan slacks and a blouse. In other circumstances she might have been beautiful, but she was involved in a process that evaluated people in terms of skills and numbers.

Johnson smiled warmly at her, but she did not look up from the computer screen as he sat down in the chair beside the desk.

"Bill Johnson?" she inquired. He admitted that was who he was. "Bill, not William?" she continued. He confirmed that. "You have some curious gaps in your past history. No birthdate? No parents? No schooling? No—"

"I have some curious gaps in my memory," Johnson said.

"Why is that?"

"As I noted on the questionnaire, I seem to have attacks of amnesia."

She looked at him for the first time and frowned. "Are you under treatment for this condition?"

"There doesn't seem to be anything anyone can do." It was not an answer to her question, but she didn't seem to notice.

"Well," she said, reacting to the change in her routine as much as she had earlier seemed to immerse herself in its lack of variety, "there doesn't seem much you're qualified to do."

"Perhaps something for which a lack of prior attachments might be an asset?" Johnson suggested.

She looked at her computer scope and punched a couple of keys. "You do have an unusual psychological profile: high empathy, low self-interest, high loyalty, low acquisitiveness, high trustworthiness, low—"

"Surely there's a job for somebody like that."

She gave him a quick suspicious glance and pushed more keys. "Your written responses would have to be checked by professional psychologists on our staff, of course. . . ."

"I understand."

"Because you could be falsifying your answers . . ."

"I've been totally candid."

"But you might be qualified," she said reluctantly, "for a special position that we've been asked to fill." She looked at him defiantly before her expression began to soften in the face of his calm concern. "We do get people who try to fake the questionnaires," she said. "It doesn't work. Not for long, anyway. We have ways to cross-check everything. But the official information about you in the social security and credit files doesn't contradict your statements."

"Aren't those confidential?" he asked innocently.

She looked at him scornfully and pressed another button. The desk began to talk to itself and then a chart unrolled from a printer beside her. She tore it off and inserted it into an envelope with a King International return and a pressure seal. "The psychologists will catch you up in any contradictions. This is to be handed to the woman at the desk down the hall—unopened."

He stood up and accepted the envelope. "May the future be kind," he said.

"Good luck," she said and smiled. It was a warm and honest smile, and it transformed her face. "Don't open the envelope," she said.

It was a test, of course—one of many. But none of them tripped him up, and neither did the psychologists to whom he talked at great length, answering their questions and taking their tests. A day later, with all his belongings, few as they were, packed into the shabby suitcase from his closet and a small advance against his salary gone to pay his back rent, he was driven in an inconspicuous brown automobile through the streets and freeways of a Los Angeles grown gray through five years of Depression but almost free of smog as industrial activity and automobile exhausts dwindled toward zero. The car was bigger on the inside than it seemed on the outside. It had a high-powered and illegal engine and a back seat that included a built-in bar, a television set, and a telephone. It also had a uniformed chauffeur who did not answer questions.

The trip continued for almost an hour in silence as they passed through a decent middle-class suburb that had survived hard times better than most. Against the foothills of the San Gabriel mountains, as the houses dwindled behind, trees began to line the road and then cluster into a small forest as they turned off the highway onto a road leading toward the mountains and what seemed like a modest ranch house.

They came to a metal gate that swung open as they approached. It was set between inconspicuous brick pillars on which small, restless cameras were almost unnoticeable, and chain-link fencing set between brick columns was invisible until one was upon it.

This was the home of Arthur King.

The King mansion was a fantasy world. Like Alice falling down the rabbit hole, vast vistas opened in front of the intruder and surprises waited around every turn. The world outside was a grim reality that gritted between the teeth; the world inside was spotless and shiny. It gleamed in Johnson's eyes as he entered so that he could only discern the outline of the uniformed guard who patted him down efficiently. And as the spotlight dimmed, the walls of the entranceway remained milkily translucent, as if they concealed secrets like a metal detector and a fluoroscope.

The flagstoned entranceway opened into a hallway that surrounded a glass-walled atrium, filled with cactus and other colorful desert plants as well as lizards and snakes and birds. It was open, apparently, to the air above, though it may have been covered by a fine mesh. Johnson had only a moment to gaze at it, however, before a door opened automatically on his left as if commanding his entrance.

Inside was a library. Except for an opening in the right wall for a door, the walls were lined with books in uniform editions. There were large leather chairs in each corner, each with a reading lamp, and against the near wall a leather sofa with a table behind it. The dominant feature of the room, however, was a massive wooden desk, so large and intricately carved in dark walnut and tooled greenish-black leather, like the furniture, that it had to be one of a kind. It even made petite the figure of the woman sitting behind it, who beckoned slowly to Johnson with her right hand upraised and her fingers curling toward her face. As Johnson approached the desk, however, he could see that the woman was not small; it was the desk that was large.

The woman was attractive but her face and body had been shaped by discipline and the habit of command. Her hair was dark with single strands of gray, her face a pattern of planes and triangles, her body tall and trim in a black, tailored dress, and her eyes like the hooded gaze of a falcon, watchful, unwavering.

"My name is Jessica," she said, as if she neither had nor needed a last name, "and I am the manager of this household. You are Johnson," she went on, as if providing for him the necessary baptismal function, "and you will be paid two hundred dollars a week after deducting the advance. Twenty-five dollars of that will be in U.S. currency, one hundred seventy-five in King scrip." Johnson opened his mouth, and she held up her hand. "Those are the same arrangements offered all new King employees. The scrip is exchangeable at King stores of all kinds and shortly is expected to be accepted at other stores. All this is academic since you will be living here—you will have a room below in the employees' quarters. You have a private bath, but you will eat in the employees' mess, also on the floor below. You will be on call twenty-four hours a day, and you will have no occasion nor need to spend money. Is that understood?"

Johnson nodded. Jessica's gray eyes appraised him before she went on, her voice not quite so peremptory. "You will be the personal assistant to Mr. King himself," she said. Her eyes glanced at the other door to the room and back to Johnson. "You will do anything Mr. King tells you to do, and, in time, anticipate his wishes before he makes them known. This will include but not be limited to carrying messages, bringing mail, fetching drinks, picking up newspapers or magazines where Mr. King may leave them, listening to Mr. King whenever he chooses to speak to you but never when he is speaking to anyone else in your presence. You will never, never touch anything on Mr. King's desk, and you will never, never, never mention to anyone anything about Mr. King or his affairs."

She did not ask this time if Johnson understood, but her gaze still was on his face and he nodded anyway.

"Mr. King has had other personal assistants who were unsatisfactory in one way or another. They all had to be gotten rid of." She did not elaborate on the fate that had befallen Johnson's predecessors, but her expression grew a bit more severe as she said the words, and it was clearly an end to be avoided.

Johnson nodded again, as if to indicate that it would not be necessary to "get rid of" him.

"It is the business of all of us to free Mr. King from the concerns of everyday living that might keep him from his great work," she said reverently. King's "great work" elicited a religious feeling from Jessica.

Johnson did not ask what that great work was.

"Mr. King's wife and daughter live with him in the living quarters on this floor, Mrs. King in the bedroom connecting with Mr. King's, Miss King on the opposite side of the atrium." From her tone Jessica did not care much for Mrs. King and even less for King's daughter. "You will address them as Mrs. King and Miss King. If either of them asks you to do something for them, you will pass the request on to another member of the household. You must be free at all times to take care of Mr. King."

Johnson nodded.

"Do you speak?" Jessica asked.

"Only when necessary."

Jessica's face thawed into a wintry smile, as if she would have been happier in a time when it was standard practice to remove the tongues of personal servants. "I think you'll do, Johnson."

"I'll do my best," he said. His smile melted Jessica's expression into something resembling spring.

"I think you will. Sally? You will show Johnson around the living quarters and then his room."

Johnson turned to the door through which he had entered the library. There, summoned by some mysterious agency, was a young woman dressed in the black uniform of a maid. When Johnson reached the door and turned back to thank Jessica, she already was busy at the desk doing something that took all her attention behind the raised tooled leather of the desk top; to her right several shelves of books had swung open to reveal the glowing screens of television and computer.

Where Jessica was all command, Sally was all sweet compliance. "That is Mr. King's bedroom," she said about the first closed door they came to on the left. "And that's Mrs. King's bedroom," she said about the second. Beyond was a large casual living room looking out upon the end of a swimming pool and beach house and beyond, a low structure that Sally said was a guest cottage.

On the other side of the atrium was a formal dining room looking out upon green lawn and trees. The next closed door was Miss King's bedroom, and the open door beyond exposed the neat order of Jessica's room.

"She doesn't have a room in the employees' quarters?" Johnson asked.

"No, sir," Sally said, her blue eyes round as if surprised at the notion that Jessica was an employee.

The front hallway had only the entranceway through which Johnson had passed and the space beside it that provided room for the guard who had frisked him and perhaps other equipment and personnel to monitor the grounds and the interior of the building. At the opposite end, past all the closed doors and the living room again, stairs had been carved from the rock of the mountainside. Down those stairs was a painted cement corridor, and a few steps beyond, another, apparently matching the hallways on the floor above.

Cut into the rock was a big kitchen and a large communal dining hall. The space under the atrium was unused, but small rooms lined each of the corridors. Johnson counted ten on each side.

His room was under Mr. King's, Sally said. In addition to the other facilities, it had an elevator that opened into Mr. King's bedroom. The elevator was small, a close fit for two people; the control panel had four buttons on it.

"There's another floor below this," Sally said. "It holds service equipment, supplies—enough food for months—rooms for the guards, and the arsenal."

"The arsenal?" Johnson repeated.

She nodded as if every house she had worked in had an arsenal.

"And the floor below that?" Johnson asked.

"There isn't any," she said.

Johnson did not ask about the purpose of the fourth button on the panel.

"Thanks," Johnson said.

"If you need anything else," she said, smiling prettily, "my room is just down the hall. Number six." As she turned away, she looked back at him as if to discover if he understood. He smiled to show that he did.

His room was not much larger than the room at the old hotel in which he had awakened, but it was cleaner. It held a twin bed, a chair upholstered in serviceable brown plastic, a reading lamp, a small wooden desk and chair, a chest of drawers, and a closet. His suitcase had already been delivered and unpacked, perhaps by the delicate white hands of Sally herself, but new clothing had been hung in the closet as if to suggest that he should put on the gray slacks, white shirt, and navy blazer.

The bathroom was small but serviceable. A woman apparently had occupied the room just before him, for the cabinet behind the bathroom mirror still held hairspray, shampoo, and makeup items. Johnson did not remove them. He took a shower and changed into the new clothes in the closet. As he finished buttoning the shirt, he turned toward the door. It was open. A young woman was standing in the doorway.

She was not much more than an adolescent, but she had the mature figure of a woman. She was dark-haired and dark-browed, and she leaned against the doorframe, ducking her head and looking up at him through her luxuriant eyelashes as she pressed her body toward him as if to make available the curves she had recently acquired.

"Hi," she said in an imitation of a sultry voice. "I'm Angel."

"You must be Miss King," Johnson said. "I'm—"

"I know who you are," she said, pouting, as if sulking because Johnson had recognized her. "You're Daddy's new assistant. I can tell you what happened to the last one."

"No thanks," Johnson said.

"It's really tough," she said in her child's voice, "trying to compete with all the free stuff that's floating around here."

"I don't think I understand," Johnson said.

"Oh, you understand, all right," Angel said, her eyes studying him insolently.

"Angel!" a sharp voice said from the corridor.

Angel turned toward the voice with irritating slowness.

"You know your father doesn't like you to come down to the employees' levels," the voice said.

"Daddy doesn't care what I do," Angel said. "You're the only one who cares. And you aren't my mother." But she slouched away, her pose as an enchantress broken now and then by the unconscious bounce of youth.

"Thank God for that!" the voice said. As Johnson moved toward the doorway, the owner of the voice came into view in the corridor. She was a woman of natural blondness and fair-skinned beauty who would have been stunningly attractive if her mouth had not been pinched with the apparent effort to keep her temper in check. "You're the new assistant, aren't you?" she asked, smiling and changing her appearance and even the lines of her slender body at the same time.

"Bill Johnson," he said.

"I'm Evangeline. Mrs. King. Please call me Evangeline."

"I've been instructed to call you Mrs. King."

"By Jessica, no doubt. Well, you can call me Mrs. King when Jessica is around but Evangeline when we're alone. And I hope we will be alone often." She smiled again. It was a friendly smile with just a touch of sensuality as if to say, "I would never consider any kind of relationship that was anything but proper—but for you I might make an exception."

Angel passed going in the other direction. "You see what I mean?" she said viciously.

Evangeline's mouth pinched again. "I have to apologize for Angel. She thinks any new man—"

But Johnson did not discover what Angel thought about new men, because just then a buzzer sounded above the bed. As he turned toward it, Evangeline said, "That's the summons of the master. You'll get used to it. I'll show you the way." She opened the door of the elevator and stood so close to the entrance that he had to brush against her as he entered. "I'd better not go up with you," she said. "Just press the top button."

He pressed the top button. The closing door shut off his

view of the beautiful woman who was not Angel's mother but the present Mrs. King, whatever number that was.

When the elevator door opened in front of Johnson, it revealed a bedroom as big as a small house. Its spaciousness dwarfed even the carved walnut custom-made bed against the far wall. The west wall was glass. Open drapes revealed a large swimming pool filled with blue water and surrounded by smooth paving. The pool was set about with chairs and tables and colorful umbrellas. Beyond the white paving was close-cropped green grass. Reflections from the pool rippled across the ceiling of the room.

The carpet was a soft beige deep pile. On it was an assortment of upholstered chairs and sofas along with lamps and tables, a small desk, and a bar with a liberally stocked cabinet behind it. Arthur King stood at the bar in shiny yellow swimming trunks and an open terrycloth jacket. His body and face were lean and tanned and youthful, and his white hair made them seem even more spectacularly young and vital. He turned from fixing himself a drink as the elevator door opened.

"You're Bill Johnson," he said warmly, striding forward and extending his right hand. "I hope we're going to be friends."

King's hand was warm and dry and strong. "I certainly hope so, Mr. King. I don't remember having any friends."

"Please," King said and smiled. "All my friends call me Art."

"I couldn't do that."

King released Johnson's hand and turned to the bar. The smile slipped unnoticed from his face, like the refrigerator light that goes out when the door is closed. "Don't mind Jessica. She lets the demands of her job overwhelm her humanity. Here," he said, picking up a glass and handing it to Johnson, "you can start by fixing me some scotch on the rocks." As Johnson took the glass and put ice cubes into it and then began pouring scotch over them, King went on. "What's this about your memory? Obviously you didn't forget how to talk or eat or how to do things like fixing a drink."

Johnson held out the glass to King. "Just personal matters. As if I had made a turn into another reality where my memories of who I was or what I have done don't belong. Or as if I was reborn into another world, full-grown but without any memories of how I got here."

"Has it happened before?"

Johnson smiled. "I don't remember. But there is some evidence that it has."

"Then it might happen again."

Johnson nodded. "If it does, I hope you will be patient with me."

"Have you tried to retrace your past?"

Johnson shook his head. "It isn't as if I have fugitive memories waiting to be restimulated. I have no memories at all. Meeting people I had known before would be like meeting strangers. I have the feeling that I might as well build a new life."

King sat down on the edge of the desk and raised his glass as if to toast Johnson's unusual condition. "So. It's just like starting with a blank slate. You can write anything you want." Johnson nodded. "I like that," King said. His face seemed almost wistful. "Sometimes I wish I could do it." Then his face firmed into its customary appearance of resolution, and he looked like the richest man in the world again. "But not for long." He took a long sip from his glass.

"I wouldn't think so," Johnson said. "You're doing something important."

King looked up a bit too quickly. "What's that? Oh, you mean putting people back to work."

"And everybody is grateful."

King shook his head. "They'll soon forget. Gratitude is the emotion of the hour; love is for the day. Hatred lasts all life long." He looked appraisingly at Johnson. "But if anyone has the means to help these days, he ought to do it."

"Not everybody feels that way."

"They should," King said. "They should. Anyway, it's only a beginning. After we get to know each other better, maybe I'll tell you the rest of it. It's hard to find somebody to talk to, you know. Almost everybody wants something from you or wants you to do something."

The door to the hallway opened and Angel entered the room. She was wearing a white bathing suit with lace around the top and bottom, and she carried a white terrycloth robe. She walked like a little girl now and spoke in a little girl's voice. "Hello, Daddy. Ready for our swim?"

"Is it that time already? Angel, this is Bill Johnson."

Angel smiled at Johnson coquettishly. "We've already met."

"I'll bet you have," King said. He spoke to Johnson as if Angel weren't present. "My daughter is like many girls deprived of their fathers by divorce or death or the demands of a career."

"Daddy!" Angel said.

King went on. "She wants the attention of every man she meets, and she's willing to do anything to get it. Anything."

"Daddy!" Angel said, close to tears.

"My friends and associates know this," King said, reaching out to pull his daughter close to him, "and give her the attention she craves without making her pay the price."

Johnson nodded as if to acknowledge the words without necessarily agreeing with them.

The door into the next bedroom opened, and Evangeline stood in the doorway looking coolly beautiful in a pale green summer dress.

"My wife," King said, "on the other hand, knows that she is the center of attention wherever she goes, but she likes the effect she has on men and the effect their attentions have on me. And she likes to prove to Angel that beside her mature charms Angel's adolescent whoring doesn't stand a chance."

"Oh, Daddy!" Angel said despairingly, but she hugged her father tightly around the waist.

King turned. "Come on, Angel," he said with rough affection, and slapped her on the bottom as he turned toward the patio door. "Let's have our swim."

Evangeline looked after them with a trace of a smile on her beautiful lips. "Welcome to our happy family, Mr. Johnson," she said.

The next few days settled into a routine in which Johnson was slipped into the King family life like a precision-ground gear, meshing smoothly with everyone else, making the whole machine work. Angel and Evangeline attempted to recruit him, each in her own way, in the no-holds-barred battle for King's favor. But Johnson indicated that he not only was neutral but, as far as they were concerned, neuter as well. King seemed to enjoy the competition, as if it were a game he played to take his mind off a more important competition elsewhere, and he even incited them to greater efforts. With Johnson, on the other hand, he was always charismatic, as if Johnson's opinion mattered because he had no involvements.

With Jessica, King behaved differently. When he spoke to her he used short, brisk sentences without emotion, as if this were the businessman who had accumulated a monumental fortune. Every morning after an early swim and breakfast while he read newspapers beside the pool, he spent a couple of hours in the study with Jessica. Johnson was never present, but occasionally he would see them together behind the desk, studying the computer, participating in a televised conference, or discussing weighty matters in hushed voices.

King would emerge from the study looking grim to eat lunch with his daughter or his wife, sometimes both. Frequently he would ask Johnson to join them and Johnson would be a spectator at the baiting that constituted their principle mode of intercourse. In the afternoon King read a mystery novel or spy thriller, swam for half an hour, napped in the big bed, rising refreshed for several scotches in the living room before dinner, bantering with his wife and daughter, chatting with Johnson, and eating dinner formally in the big dining room with his family and Jessica. Johnson was not invited to join them for dinner, but afterward King watched a film in the study, where one panel rolled down to expose a screen and another panel opened to expose a projector, with whoever wanted to watch invited, including Johnson. He was in bed by eleven.

Twice the routine was disturbed by the arrival of a young man, a different one each time, each admitted in the late afternoon and spending more than an hour in the study with King and Jessica. One of them had hurried away immediately afterward, but the other stayed for the social hour and dinner.

King introduced him as Doug France.

"And this," Doug said, raising his glass to King, "is the next President of the United States."

"That's enough!" Jessica said in her most peremptory tone of command.

King grinned. "Now, Doug, you know I'm going to turn it down." He looked boyishly modest and at the same time a man of wisdom and mature judgment.

"All the same," Doug said stubbornly, "you're what this country needs—and the world, too."

Johnson turned to King. "Are you thinking of running for President, Mr. King?"

"That's none of your business!" Jessica snapped.

"Now, Jessica," King said. "Bill is one of the family."

"You must not have been watching television," Evangeline said lightly. "It's been on all the news. Both party conventions are coming up in the next couple of weeks, and party leaders on both sides have talked of nominating Art as their candidate."

King laughed. He seemed to be enjoying the discussion. "That's because I've been smart enough never to become involved in politics, and when I've made contributions to candidates I've always given equal amounts to each side."

"Gee, Daddy," Angel said, "would you be the first candidate ever nominated by both parties?"

"Eisenhower might have had it if he hadn't identified himself as a Republican before the conventions," King said. "But he was a war hero."

"It's better to be a peace hero, darling," Evangeline said.

"No man is a hero to his valet," King said ironically,

smiling at Johnson. "Nor to his wife," he added, looking at Evangeline. "Or to his daughter," he continued, turning his gaze toward Angel.

Each of them looked injured but unwilling to admit it by protesting their admiration for King, as if by restraining their natural impulses they could deny his power to hurt them.

"In any case," King went on, looking at Doug, "it's all academic. Politics is not for me. Campaigning, making promises, concessions, compromises. . . ."

"To the good old days!" Doug said, raising his glass again.

"What days were those?" Johnson asked.

"You know—when things were done properly—" Doug began.

"Shut up, Doug!" Jessica said.

"Bill doesn't remember the good old days," King said. "Nor any old days, for that matter. That is his charm . . ."

For once, Johnson was invited to join the family for dinner, perhaps to make up, with Doug, an even table. The conversation was a strange mixture of overtones and undertones, with political talk mingling with King's customary teasing of his wife and daughter. King's cruelty to them contrasted oddly with his kindness to Johnson and his careful directness with Jessica. Doug he treated as a subordinate to be ordered about. The political discussions, on the other hand, though they seemed to be about other candidates, appeared to carry innuendos that Johnson was not supposed to understand.

At one point when the others were engrossed in a conversation of their own, Evangeline, seated next to him, leaned over and said softly, "Art really would like to be President, you know."

"Why?"

She looked at her husband at the far end of the table with a mixture of pride, love, and bewilderment. "He has so much to give, so many things this world needs—leadership, direction. . . ." Her voice trailed off.

"What direction?"

"I don't know," she said. "He doesn't talk about such things with me."

"Darling," King said lightly from the other end of the table, "there's no use in your trying to seduce Bill. He's already proved himself impervious to your charms."

Evangeline looked pained and her jaw tightened as if she were holding in a reply.

"Anyway," King continued, "think how damaging it would be to your self-esteem to make love to a man who doesn't remember you afterward." He chuckled, and the others joined in the laughter as if to deny the cruel edge to his remarks.

Afterward, with the others gone, King turned to Johnson in the bedroom as Johnson was pulling the drapes to shut out the night. "The world's in a sorry mess," he said, clinking ice cubes in his glass.

"Yes, sir," Johnson replied. "I guess there's a lot of things wrong."

"It's not just the economy," King went on, almost as if he were talking to himself. "That's just one of the symptoms. It's politics, cynicism, loss of faith, confusion of values. 'Things fall apart,' " he quoted.

" 'The center cannot hold,' " Johnson continued.

"You remember that?" King asked.

"I've been doing some reading in my room," Johnson said. "I've borrowed a few books from your library. I hope you don't mind."

CRISIS!

King waved his hand as if he had already forgotten. "There are times when the world is served best by weak government that allows natural leaders to build and develop, the economy to grow, the people to prosper. But there are times when strong leadership is crucial. When competing theories of history try to guide the world into the future along one channel or another."

"But what can we do?"

"We need a leader who is willing to meet force with greater force, to call people to the service of something greater than themselves, to be firm, strong, confident, bold. And all we have is little men without vision or purpose, seeking little advantages for themselves or their constituents while they let the great issues pass them by without blinking."

"What about you, sir?" Johnson asked.

King shrugged. "What can one man do?"

"But you have a chance to be nominated. To be President. Surely as President you could put your philosophy into action."

King looked speculatively into the glass of scotch and ice cubes he held in his hand. "Do you realize how difficult it is to move the great hulk of government? Congress? The entrenched bureaucracies? The courts? One man doesn't have a chance to put anything into action. It's all he can do to move the behemoth an inch or two one way or another."

"Surely there are ways," Johnson said, "to cut through the red tape? Go around the behemoth?"

King glanced at Johnson. "Can you keep a secret?"

Johnson smiled. "That's what I'm best at."

"Yes, of course," King said, looking into the depths of his glass again as if it were a crystal ball. "There is a way.

It would involve a radical change in our way of government at least for the duration of the crisis. A temporary delegation of authority to the executive. A temporary limitation on the authority of the courts."

Johnson looked thoughtfully at King. "Wouldn't that be dangerous?"

"Yes," King agreed. He leaned back against the desk. "But not to act is dangerous, too. Maybe more dangerous. You have to trust the executive. His ability to operate the government like a well-run business. From the top. Making decisions. Delegating authority. Seeing his orders carried out or replacing the foolish and incompetent with those who *will* carry them out. There's precedent, you know. That's what we do in wartime. And we are in a kind of war. Maybe a condition more urgent than war."

"What if it didn't work?" Johnson asked. "What if he failed?"

"Would we be any worse off? But he wouldn't fail. Not if he's the right kind of person who knows what has to be done and how to do it." King's face was animated; his voice was excited.

"And what if he succeeded," Johnson said, "but saw another problem ahead and another that needed his unusual abilities and his extraordinary powers? Would he want to give up his control of things? Just when events were moving in the right direction? Would we ever get democracy again?"

Their voices seemed hushed in the big, soft room.

"You've got to have confidence in your leaders," King said. "George Washington could have been king; he refused even the trappings. Anyway, democracy doesn't exist in institutions but in people. As long as people believe in democracy it will continue. The danger is in

CRISIS! 115

their loss of faith. If it proves inadequate. . . ." His voice trailed off into silence. "But that's all hypothetical," he said finally.

"You're turning down the nomination tomorrow?"

King smiled slyly. "You'll have to wait and see. Like everyone else. Just because you're my personal assistant—I'm only teasing, Bill. I like you. You're easy to talk to. I bet people tell you things."

"I guess they do."

"Like talking to a priest," King muttered. He studied Johnson's face. "Because you don't talk, and chances are you're going to forget."

" 'And what rough beast, its hour come round at last,' " Johnson said, " 'slouches toward Bethlehem to be born?' "

"You remember that, eh?"

"Yes, sir. Will there be anything else?"

"Not tonight," King said wearily. He looked tired. " 'What rough beast,' " he muttered, and turned his hands palm upward and studied them as if he expected to find stigmata.

The library was crowded with people and television equipment. All the furniture had been removed from the room except the big desk and the chair behind it. The door to the hall and the door into King's bedroom stood open. People kept coming and going through the doorway into the hall, but nobody entered the bedroom where King and Jessica remained in conference.

One of the members of the television crew was Robert Scott, his stony face rigid above the gray collar of the King International uniform. He was tinkering with the control panel when he looked up and saw Johnson. Johnson was walking toward Scott when King appeared in the bedroom door and said, "Bill, why don't you get these men some beer and soft drinks. This is hot work."

"Yes, sir," Johnson said, and members of the crew murmured their appreciation for King's thoughtfulness.

Johnson motioned Scott to follow him as he passed. He led the way down the hallway to the stairs and down the stairs to the kitchen. He relayed the order for drinks to the kitchen crew and then walked quickly down the corridor to his room. As he entered he motioned to Scott for silence, walked to the elevator, opened the door, and gestured to Scott to join him. Scott's normally impassive features were curious, but he slipped in beside Johnson. Johnson pushed the bottom button.

The ride was long. Finally the car stopped and the door opened. In front of them was a large, concrete room. At the far end was a corridor with doors opening off it on either side. The place had the feel of a bunker far below ground, but it had been maintained. The paved floor was not dusty. Air whispered through ceiling ducts. Automatic rifles racked against the wall were clean. Machine guns and mortars in rows upon the floor gleamed with oil. Boxes of ammunition and grenades were stacked neatly against the walls.

"This is a god-damned arsenal!" Scott exclaimed.

"Only part of it," Johnson said. "The small arms are on the floor above. But that's not why I brought you here."

"What are you doing here?" Scott asked, stepping out of the elevator, half-distracted by the sight of all the weapons.

"That's not important either. But I got a job as personal assistant to King, just as you got a job with his communications section."

CRISIS! 117

"But you're in a perfect position to— How did you know that?"

"About your job? Isn't it obvious?"

Their voices echoed off the hard walls.

"I guess. We've got to talk."

"Talk fast. There are no cameras or bugs here. But our absence mustn't be noticed."

"You know what King is up to, don't you?"

"The Presidency?"

"His name will be put in nomination at the upcoming Republican convention. If he doesn't get that, he'll be nominated by the Democrats." He couldn't seem to get his eyes off the blue metal.

"Or both."

"Both?" Scott looked quickly at Johnson. "Yes, of course. Why didn't I think of that? He's got to be stopped."

"Why?" Johnson asked simply.

"People already are calling him King Arthur," Scott said. "He's got all the economic power. What if he had the political power, too?"

"Maybe he'd be a good President."

"What are his plans? What are his principles? What does he stand for?"

"Putting everybody back to work? Ending the Depression?"

"Building a political base? Becoming unbeatably popular?"

"But if he were—as you put it—stopped, wouldn't that end the recovery? Throw millions out of work again? Turn joy and hope into misery and despair?"

"What good are jobs if you lose your freedom?" Scott asked.

"What good is freedom without a job?"

"The old free-enterprise–Marxist dilemma." Scott looked straight at Johnson. "I don't know what the future holds, but I do know this: King isn't what he seems. He's rising to power as a man of vision, a philanthropist who cares more about his fellow man than mere worldly possessions, a kindly man who is at the same time a superb executive—exactly what anyone would want for a President. But look at this!" Scott waved his hand at the weapons and the boxes. "That's not what a philanthropist keeps in his cellar. Those are the possessions of a man who believes in force."

"Or defense," Johnson said. "You can't fault a man who strives for the best but prepares for the worst."

"Mussolini made the Italian trains run on time and Hitler brought Germany out of its Depression. And they took us into a war that destroyed millions of people."

"Some times it is better to suffer a little evil now to avoid a greater evil later on."

"What about doing a little evil now to avoid a greater evil later on?"

"That never works. You can't know you're going to avoid the greater evil. You can only do good by doing good."

"What if someone had shot Mussolini in 1922 or Hitler in 1933?"

"You're the political scientist. Wouldn't conditions have produced someone else? Maybe somebody worse after the drama of the assassination?"

"Who can know these things?" Scott asked. Johnson sighed, but Scott went on, "King is the man of the hour. I don't think anybody can replace him."

"What are you going to do?"

Scott patted his waistband under his uniform jacket.

"How did you get it in here past the guards and the metal detectors?" Johnson asked.

"I hid it in the control panel," Scott said, "and in all the confusion nobody searched too hard."

"You mustn't do it. Nothing good will come of it."

"How do you know?"

"I know." Johnson said it with complete confidence.

Scott brushed it aside. "If you can't help, just stay out of my way. And if I fail maybe you'll have a better chance."

"What if I told you he's going to ask people not to nominate him?"

Scott looked at Johnson stunned. "Is that what he's going to do? My God! Why didn't I think of that? Just like Caesar, but Caesar turned down the crown three times. Once for King will be enough. They'll make him take it. This is all carefully planned, but all it takes is one well-placed bullet."

"There's a better way," Johnson said urgently.

"What?"

"There's always a better way."

"Oh."

"The only way King can truly be stopped," Johnson said, "is if he stops himself. He must have a chance to reveal his true nature."

"How could we do that?"

"You," Johnson said. "You must do it. Haven't there been occasions when people exposed more of themselves than they intended?" He stepped back into the elevator. Scott squeezed in beside him. Johnson pressed the second button from the top. "You'll think of something," he said.

He led the way out through his room and down the

hallway to the stairs leading to the first floor. Scott stopped suddenly and felt his waist. He started trotting after Johnson. "My—" he started. "You've—"

Johnson called back over his shoulder. "You'll think of something."

King entered the room wearing a dark-gray business suit, a pale-blue shirt, and a dark-blue tie. It looked a bit like the King International uniform but expensive. His face was bronze under his neatly combed white hair. "Good morning, boys," he called to the television crew. He went behind the big desk and talked to Jessica in a low voice, gesturing occasionally at the cameras.

"Are you going to make an announcement, Mr. King?" one of the cameramen asked.

King glanced up and smiled before going back to his low conversation. From his position in the doorway into King's bedroom, Johnson saw Scott move from the control panel as if in sudden decision, go to one of the cameras, and begin checking it.

King concluded his conversation with Jessica and turned to the cameras. He blinked into the lights. "All right, gentlemen. Are you ready?"

The director, a large, middle-aged man with an earphone and pencil microphone clamped to his head, said, "All ready, Mr. King."

"This is live, right?" King said.

"Yes, sir. When I give you the signal, the red light will come on under the camera we are using. It will be eleven A.M. here, two o'clock in New York where the networks will be taping for their evening news. But at least two of them are breaking into their regular programs to carry your statement live. How long will you be speaking, Mr. King?"

CRISIS! 121

"Just five minutes."

Members of the crew glanced at each other as if questioning the trouble of setting up all this equipment for a five-minute speech.

"You'll be sitting at your desk, right, Mr. King?" the director asked.

"I'll start seated and then get up, move to the front of the desk, and sit on the front edge, informally."

"Got that, boys?" the director asked the cameramen. "We'll have the middle camera head on, the others cheated right and left. Just watch the red light, and—"

"I know all that," King said impatiently.

"Yes, sir. It is now ten fifty-nine, if you want to get ready. I'll count down as we get to fifteen seconds."

King sat down behind the desk and composed his face. He looked serious, concerned, sympathetic. It was the face on the billboards.

"Fifteen seconds," the director said. "Ten. Nine. Eight. Seven. Six. Five. Four. Three. And you're on, Mr. King."

King looked into the center camera. "Hello, friends," he said. "I'm Arthur King and I'm speaking to you today from my home near Los Angeles." He stood up and moved around the desk toward the front. He did it with the ease of an experienced actor, but it looked effortless and unstudied. "In a misguided effort to provide leadership in these troubled times, a few people have put my name forward as a possible candidate for President of the United States. I want you to know that I am not a candidate."

Scott looked up from the control panel toward Johnson.

"I am not a political person," King went on, "in spite of the fact that my business activities often involve me in concerns and decisions that not only deal with the political process but often involve the same kind of give-and-take as legislation and the effective use of resources that is involved in administration."

He leaned back against the edge of the desk and smiled modestly. "I am an industrialist, though I was born of working parents. I have worked all my life. I have also been blessed by good fortune. No one gets to the position I hold on merit alone. Now, through the worldwide branches of the enterprises I head, I find myself negotiating with prime ministers and heads of state of all kinds, the way I used to deal with supervisors and shop foremen and grocery clerks. And"—he leaned forward confidentially toward the camera and smiled—"I can tell you it isn't much different."

He allowed himself a self-deprecating chuckle.

"I am neither a Republican nor a Democrat. I have held no political office, and I want none. I have quite enough to do managing the businesses for which I am responsible—and seeing that our new employees, who now number more than ten million, are usefully occupied and paid on time."

King smiled benignly.

"I will not be so vain nor so insensible to the opinions of others as to say, as a famous general once said, 'If nominated I will not run; if elected I will not serve.' I do not expect to be nominated by either party, and I urge those who are mentioning my name not to do so, to turn to others who are better qualified by position and temperament and experience."

He rested himself on the top of the desk and crossed his ankles.

"I suppose there are conditions under which I would respond to a genuine draft, but they are so unlikely that even mentioning them would be tantamount to doing a

Sherman. I allude to this only to let you all know that I do not place myself above the office or the needs of this nation or the world. It is simply that I cannot imagine—or imagine anyone believing for a moment—that I am the only person who can do what needs to be done."

He stared into the camera lens sincerely for a long moment and then said, "Thank you, and may God be with you."

He held his gaze on the lens until the red light went out, and then turned to Jessica who moved toward him with a quick, triumphant skip. His face changed to an expression almost sly, and he said, "If they believe that, they'd believe anything."

It was said as a mutter to be heard only by Jessica, but the words seemed to boom out. They were followed by an awful moment of silence. Everyone looked at each other.

"But the red light went out!" King said.

The director's face had turned pale. "It must have malfunctioned."

"The camera was still on," Scott said.

"You mean that went out on the air?" King asked as if in pain.

"I'm afraid so," the director said. "Just a minute. I'll check."

"Never mind," King said. His face had become set and gray under its tan. He turned and went toward his bedroom door. His walk was unsteady as if he were drunk or had aged twenty years. Jessica trotted after him, attempting to clutch his arm, but he brushed her hand away and stopped her from following him.

Johnson had moved from the doorway to the bar and quickly fixed King a drink. As he handed him the glass, the onetime man of the hour said to himself, "Gone. All gone. All in a second." He drained the glass in one long swallow.

Evangeline came through the doorway and stopped beside King. Her face was compassionate and loving in a way it had not been before. King's arm came out and brought her close to him in an unconscious gesture of need. "Vangy," he said. "Thank God you're here."

Then he saw his daughter standing in front of him, and he reached out with his other arm and hugged her close as well. "Angel," he said huskily. "We've got to get to know each other, we three."

"May the future be kind," Johnson said.

Johnson looked around his small room as if searching for something. Then he shook his head and went into the bathroom. Finally he opened the mirrored medicine cabinet door. On a shelf with hairspray, shampoo, eye shadow, and other cosmetics was a small, cylindrical metal case. Johnson removed the cap and screwed the base until a red, waxy material protruded from the top. He closed the cabinet door and began to write upon the mirror in small, precise letters.

"Your name is Bill Johnson," he wrote. "You have stopped a man from becoming a dictator and ending a great experiment in democracy, and you don't remember. You may find the newspapers filled with reports of what happened, but you will find no mention of the part you played.

"For this there are several possible explanations. . . ."

After he had finished, he tossed the container into the wastebasket, turned off the light, and went to his bed. He lay down with his hands behind his head, staring up at the ceiling, and waited for the night.

Episode Four
Touch of the Match

The room was illuminated only by the feeble glow of a night light through the open door of a white-tiled bathroom. The man lying quietly on his back, his arms extended beside his body outside the covers, opened his eyes and stared blankly at the ceiling. His eyes blinked once and then twice quickly and then he threw back the covers and sat up, swinging his legs over the side of the narrow bed, and put his face into his upturned palms.

It was a good face, brown and well-formed, but now it was blank as if all the character shaped by a lifetime of crises and decisions had been erased from it. The man lowered his hands and stood up carefully. He walked to the glow of the bathroom and turned on the light. He tried to look at his face in the mirror over the lavatory, like a man trying to verify his identity after a bad night, but the mirror was covered with small, precise red letters. The man refocused his eyes on them.

"Your name is Bill Johnson," the letters said. "You have stopped a man from becoming a dictator and ending a great experiment in democracy, and you don't remember. You may find the newspapers filled with reports of what happened, but you will find no mention of the part you played.

"For this there are several possible explanations, including the likelihood that I may be lying or deceived or insane. But the explanation on which you must act is that I have told you the truth: you are a man who was born in a future that has almost used up all hope; you were sent to this time and place to alter the events that created that future.

"Am I telling the truth? The only evidence you have is your apparently unique ability to foresee consequences—it comes like a vision, not of the future because the future can be changed, but of what will happen if events take their natural course, if someone does not act, if you do not intervene.

"But each time you intervene, no matter how subtly, you change the future from which you came. You exist in this time and outside of time and in the future, and so each change makes you forget.

"I wrote this message last night to tell you what I know, just as I learned about myself a few days ago by listening to a recording in a used-record shop, for I am you and we are one, and we have done this many times before."

The man stared at the message for several minutes, his face slowly changing from comprehension to understanding to acceptance, and then he took a washcloth from a rack beside the lavatory, moistened it from the hot water tap, and wiped the mirror clean. He stared down at the red smears on the cloth for a moment as if wishing that he

CRISIS! 127

could wipe other things away as easily and then tossed it into the clothes hamper in the corner.

After he had showered and dressed in the oldest clothing he found in the closet of the windowless room, he put into his pockets a small heap of belongings from the top of the small dresser. They included a few coins, a black pocket comb, and a billfold. In the billfold were a Visa credit card, three one-dollar bills and a five in U.S. currency, and one hundred seventy-five dollars in twenty-five-dollar bills printed in black, yellow, and red and labeled "King International Scrip." In the center of the bills was a full-color picture of a man with white hair but a strong, tanned, and youthful face. Underneath the picture a legend said, "Arthur King."

The man put his few belongings into an old suitcase he found in the closet. He left hanging in the closet a navy blazer and a pair of gray slacks that seemed to go with them, and made his way down a gray concrete corridor lined with closed doors on one side and a solid wall on the other, past a busy dining room and kitchen that seemed to have been carved out of rock, and up a flight of stairs to a well-lighted living area. In front of him was a glass-walled atrium. On either side of the atrium was a wide hallway. Doors opened off the hallway on either side. The atrium was bright with morning sun and filled with sand and cactus, snakes, lizards, and birds, and other desert creatures.

The man paused, as if he would have liked to have stopped and watched the atrium scene, but at the far end of the hall, where one might expect to find a front door, men were busy with some kind of construction work, and he went toward them. As he passed the open doorway of a room filled with books, a woman with a face like an arrangement of chisels and anvils looked up from the enormous desk she sat behind. "Johnson?" she said. "Where do you think you're sneaking off to?"

Johnson put his suitcase down beside the door and stepped into the room. "Whatever I've been doing here," he said in a gentle, well-modulated voice, "has come to an end. I belong somewhere else."

"You'll go when we tell you it's time to go—" she began, and was interrupted by the opening of the door to her left.

A tall, white-haired man stood in the doorway. He wore a blue robe that looked as if it had cost as much as some men's suits. His face was the one pictured on the King International scrip, but it was softer in real life, less touched by destiny, more reconciled with life as it is. He evaluated the scene at a glance. "Johnson?" he said. "You're leaving us?"

"He thinks he's leaving," the woman said.

"If Bill wants to leave, that's his right," the white-haired man said, "but I hope he won't." The woman looked scornful. "Oh, I know, Jessica, you still hold Bill responsible for the collapse of our presidential hopes, but that's folly. He was nowhere near any of the equipment. No, it was my own stupidity. I cut my own throat. I'm just sorry I cut yours in the process. It's too bad. We would have made a good President, you and I."

The brief expression of wistfulness passed from his face, and he turned to Johnson. "It's happened again?"

"Yes, Mr. King."

"But you know my name."

"It was on the scrip."

"Of course," King said. "You know you're welcome to stay, to pick up what you've forgotten."

"That wouldn't be fair to those who have memories of

relationships or to those who would have to instruct me again in everything I was supposed to have learned. It's better for me to be among strangers."

"It's a hard world out there," King said. "A man needs friends and walls to protect him. There's a lot of passion in the world, a lot of hatred, a lot of angry people with bombs and weapons in their hands. I thought maybe I could do something about it, but it wasn't to be."

" 'The best lack all conviction,' " Johnson quoted, " 'while the worst are full of passionate intensity.' "

"You remember Yeats?" King said.

"It's just Johnson I forget."

"I can see there isn't any stopping you."

"There's always a way," Jessica said.

"I used to think that," King said. "Now I'm not so sure. I think there are some things we must accept the way they are. And maybe that's best. We can relax, enjoy life, people. Angel and Evangeline will miss you. I know you don't remember them, but Evangeline is my wife and Angel is my daughter, and they are very fond of you."

"Tell them good-bye for me," Johnson said. And he turned to the door and picked up his battered suitcase and walked down the corridor and out the front door past the workmen who were putting armorplate coated with imitation wood on the outer door. Beyond, other men were building a heavy metal entranceway.

"What's that?" Johnson asked.

King answered from the doorway behind him. "That's one of those new anti-bomb devices. Radio waves detonate any kind of chemical explosive. When these get installed all over the world, it will take care of the terrorists for sure."

Johnson looked through the tunnel formed by the device

as if he could see far down it to a vision at the end of the world. "I hope so," he said. "Civilization depends on trust. Without trust there may be no future."

King looked at the construction and smiled. "Not as long as people are strong."

"Or sensible," Johnson said. "May the future be kind."

The Los Angeles airport had been fortified. Barbed wire encircled the entire perimeter, and tank traps had been placed wherever it was possible for an automobile or a truck to approach a runway or a building. All incoming vehicles had to park far from the terminal, and the passengers were transported to their airlines in electric buses that passed through metal tunnels—larger versions of the entranceway Johnson had seen being built to King's residence—and even the electric carts and trucks that dashed around the airport itself were funneled through similar devices on the field.

Johnson studied it all as he made his way by bus and foot to the counter where he bought his ticket and had to sign a form swearing that he had read the list of materials that would explode, and that he had none of them on his person or in his luggage, and a waiver of responsibility for damage to body or property that might be caused by such explosions. He also had an opportunity to purchase temporary insurance against any of these contingencies. That application he threw away.

He and his bag passed through a series of devices without incident, and he found himself on an airplane sitting in the middle seat of three on the right of the aisle. On his right was a pretty, dark-haired young woman who seemed to be frightened at the prospect of taking off. On his left was a dark-haired, brown-faced young man who seemed nervous for some other reason.

Johnson turned to the woman on his right as the plane engines began to roar and the plane picked up speed slowly for its takeoff. "First time?" he asked. She nodded, apparently unwilling or unable to speak. "Don't worry," he said. "Everything will be all right."

"It's not the airplane I'm afraid of," she said breathlessly. "It's the people on it."

"They've all been checked," he said. "There's nothing to worry about."

"There always are things to worry about these days," she said. "Every time you leave the house you worry whether some crazy fanatic will blow you up before you return. Not because he hates you. Just because you're there. And if you don't leave home you still worry. Lying in bed at night. Maybe the car engine you hear at night that stops near your house is a bomb waiting to go off."

"Then you can feel safer here," Johnson said.

"They're clever," she said. "They always seem to find a way of getting around everything."

As if that were a signal—though it was more likely the fact that the plane was committed to flight—the brown-faced man beside Johnson sprang to his feet and held his right hand threateningly in the air. "Nobody move!" he said with a Middle Eastern accent. "I have bomb. It go off if this plane no go to Teheran!" The last word he said so well that it was almost incomprehensible.

One of the flight attendants approached the man from the front of the cabin. "Now," she said soothingly, "you know you don't have a bomb. Just sit down, and we will be in Washington before you know it. You can get a flight there to Teheran."

"I have gun," the dark-complexioned man said.

"Now, you know you don't have a gun," the attendant said with professional calm. "You can't get a gun through the detectors."

A male flight attendant moved up behind the hijacker but made no attempt to seize him.

"I have new bomb!" the hijacker said desperately. "No set off."

"You know that's not true," the attendant in front said. She reached out a hand to turn him back toward his seat. Defeated, the would-be hijacker turned and allowed the attendant behind him to help him into his seat beside Johnson.

"I fail," the dark-complexioned man said disconsolately and then spoke a few rapid words in a foreign language. He stared down at his hands clasped helplessly in his lap.

"What kind of person would try something like that, anyway?" the girl by the window demanded, her voice breaking from tension.

"He must be a person under a great deal of stress," Johnson said.

"That's no excuse!" the girl said angrily.

"I fail," the man said again. "I die."

Johnson spoke to him quietly, to the indignation of the girl by the window and perhaps, by the shufflings around him, to the indignation of everyone within earshot. For a long time, while the airplane rose above the mountains and soared above the desert, the man didn't respond. Then, finally, he began to talk to Johnson in his broken English, and the tragic story of his life emerged.

Born a displaced Palestinian, he had grown up in the squalor of Lebanese camps. His mother had been killed by

Israeli bombs, and his father and brothers had given their lives in terrorist activities when he was twelve, leaving only him and his sister. He had joined a fundamentalist Iranian group pledged to martyrdom, but he had been weak. He had been concerned about his sister's welfare. With the help of the organization, he had been slipped into this country with forged papers in order to blow up important installations or government buildings when he was given instructions, but really he had tried to get a job so that he could send money to his sister in Lebanon.

But there were no good jobs and little money, and when the instructions came he was afraid—not so much for himself, he wanted Johnson to understand, but what would his sister do if there were no money at all?

Finally, there was nothing to do but to try to return. He had no money for airfare, and his terrorist comrades would not welcome him back with his assignment unfulfilled, but perhaps if he returned with an airplane of the Great Satan it would be considered an honorable act, and if he died in the attempt perhaps the group would care for his sister.

"Can there be no end to the killing?" Johnson asked.

"Not till there be justice."

"What kind of justice?"

"We get back our land."

"What is justice to one may be injustice to another."

"Let others suffer."

"Their suffering would lead only to acts of desperation such as yours. More violence. More terrorism, this time against you rather than yours against them."

"Then there be no end, even with justice." The Palestinian accepted that outcome fatalistically as if everything could end in blood and destruction and he would not complain.

"What if the Palestinians were given other land?"

"Where is land to give away? No matter. It not be Palestine."

"What if it were better? What if Palestinians could come to this country like the Vietnamese, could have jobs, could make new lives for themselves."

"It not be Palestine. For me, maybe good. For my sister, yes. For others there still be hatred. Those would not come; their anger be watered, or they be dirtied by the Great Satan, or if they come it be only to destroy."

Johnson looked toward the window on his right. It had been a long conversation that had lasted through lunch, and the airplane was descending into Dulles Airport. Green hills were visible, and dark clouds could be seen mounting into thunderheads far to the south.

When Johnson raised his eyes, the girl in the window seat was looking at him. She was frowning. "You see?" she said. "There's no use talking to them."

Before Johnson could reply, the plane leveled off and made a right turn. The speakers above their heads offered the peculiar hush that always preceded an announcement, and then an authoritative voice said, "This is Captain Bradley, folks. We're going to have to delay our descent into Dulles Airport for a few minutes, and we'll be circling in a holding pattern along with all the other planes about to land. This has been an eventful flight, but there's nothing to be alarmed about. It seems that the space shuttle was committed to a landing at Cape Canaveral when an unexpected thunderstorm sprang up along the Florida coast. Those passengers on the left side of the plane can see the thunderstorm if they look far to the south. The shuttle has been diverted to Dulles, and all traffic has been delayed until it lands. It should be an occasion. Maybe we'll get a glimpse of it as it comes—*there it is!*" The captain's voice was suddenly excited, before it descended again to its customary calm. "Those passengers on the right can see it—a speck of white at two o'clock. Passengers on the left may be able to pick it up soon. . . ."

And so it was that they were allowed to land shortly after the incredible white delta-shaped machine had preceded them by a few minutes into the airport. The passengers cheered and clapped, as if they had forgotten for a wonderful moment the terror in which they lived. Even the Palestinian beside Johnson had craned his neck for a look at the shuttle.

The terror began again after they had been herded into several of the tall vehicles that were intended to ferry them between plane and terminal. Midway, the vehicle that was carrying Johnson and his seatmates and some fifty other passengers made a gentle arc whose purpose was not perceived until one of the passengers saw the terminal out of the right-hand windows and said, "We're heading the wrong way."

A babble of voices, rising in volume and querulousness, began shouting questions. People turned in their seats to look out the windows and some of them got up and looked toward the front where two uniformed figures were half hidden in the control cubicle.

As the noise level increased, one of them turned, opened the glass door, and stepped into the passenger area. "All be silent!" the person shouted. It seemed like a woman's voice, though it was hard to tell, because it was husky and the accent was foreign. The figure fumbled at its belt and then pulled free a black knifelike object. The figure held it up threateningly. "Silence!" the person warned.

One of the flight attendants stepped forward. It was the same one who had dealt with the Palestinian on the plane. "There's no use threatening us with that. You can't hold off all of us." The noise level had dropped so that the attendant's words were heard by everyone.

"I kill many," the terrorist said quietly, and the words were more frightening for their lack of intensity. Clearly it was a woman's voice, and that was more frightening yet. The flight attendant took a step closer and a few of the bolder passengers behind surged forward. "You I kill first," the terrorist said to the flight attendant. The flight attendant tried to shrink back but was unable to retreat more than a step because of the bodies behind her.

The terrorist waved her dagger at the mass of them. "If you attack and not die, my comrade crash bus. This bus not go fast but fast enough, and if raised crash do injury to many." As if in response to her words, the body of the vehicle began to elevate itself from the ground. The balance seemed to shift from side to side as if it were about to overturn, and people shrank back into their seats to keep it stable. The flight attendant retreated to a seat at the far end and seemed willing to have someone else assume responsibility.

Johnson stepped forward. "No one is going to do anything rash—"

"Appeaser!" said the woman who had been seated beside him in the airplane. "Terrorist-lover!"

The terrorist waved her knife at the woman. "You! Come!" She motioned the woman forward.

"No," the young woman said faintly, trying to fade into her seat.

"You!" The terrorist rapped once on the glass door behind her. The vehicle turned and leaned, turned back and leaned in the other direction. The passengers tensed and tried to keep the mobile lounge from tipping over by shifting their weight to the opposite side. "You!" the terrorist repeated. "Come!"

The young woman shrank back, but the passengers around her pushed her forward until she stood, trying to retreat, beside Johnson. "Don't be afraid," Johnson said, taking her arm reassuringly. "You won't be hurt."

"You not be hurt," the terrorist said in her husky voice, "if you do as told—if all do as told. You—hostage. You and you," she said, indicating Johnson and the young woman. "If any move wrong, these die first." She reached up with her left hand and removed her uniform cap. Black hair fell around her shoulders. Now there was no mistaking her sex. She was a beautiful woman, even though her face was set in an expression of savage determination.

"Fatima!" a foreign voice said from among the passengers. The Palestinian who had talked so long to Johnson stood up and started forward, hands half raised as if beholding an apparition.

"Fatima?" the Palestinian said again.

The woman had raised her dagger in quick alarm. "You know my name? How—?" And then, "Mohammed? It be you?"

They both spoke rapidly in a foreign language as they approached. A sequence of emotions crossed their faces. The Palestinian called Mohammed was about to embrace the woman he had called Fatima when she stepped back and motioned with her dagger at the passengers. "I always ready," she said. "Not do anything." She stepped forward and put her arms around Mohammed.

"That man is under arrest," the flight attendant said. "He tried to hijack the plane to Teheran."

Fatima's face brightened. "Ah, Mohammed! You try!"

Mohammed looked despondent. "I fail."

"He's still under arrest," the flight attendant said.

"No more," Fatima said proudly. "My brother go with me. He freedom fighter like me."

The mobile lounge slowed, and she stepped back from her brother. The compartment lurched as the lounge turned. Through the forward windows Johnson could see the white bulk of the space shuttle. When, as the mobile lounge passed the shuttle's tail, it came into the view of the seated passengers on the right, some of them gasped and others began to talk excitedly.

"You and you!" Fatima said to Johnson and the young woman. "Out!" She motioned toward the front of the vehicle. After they had passed, she reached down and took another plastic dagger from her boot. She handed it to Mohammed. "You follow! Guard!" She turned to the other passengers. "Far to ground. Anybody move, these die. You be killer." The lounge had stopped with its front pressed to the left side of the shuttle.

The shuttle, still warm from its passage through the resisting air, stood at the end of a white runway marked by the black skid marks of innumerable airplane wheels that had touched down there in the years since the airport had been in use. They stood with their faces close to the radiating white tiles. The shuttle looked much bigger than it had looked from the air.

A dark-faced young man in uniform emerged from the control booth beside them and knocked sharply on the shuttle's side. A crack appeared in the tile and widened into a squared oval of darkness. A middle-aged man in astronaut's uniform appeared in the entranceway blinking in the sunlight. As he moved onto the lounge's platform, the young man who had knocked moved back into the control booth and pushed something. The lounge began lowering.

"What's happening?" the astronaut asked.

"But that's Henry Chrisman," the young woman beside Johnson said almost simultaneously.

As both sets of words still seemed to hang in the air the woman called Fatima had moved beside the astronaut and placed the tip of her dagger under his chin and her left hand on the man's shoulder so that he could not draw back. "Not resist! No move quick. No one get hurt."

The lounge had reached the ground. "Come!" Fatima commanded, leading Chrisman forward. Johnson and the others followed as Fatima motioned to Mohammed to bring them off the lounge. The lounge retreated from the shuttle's side about ten feet and then began to raise itself once more into the air. The dark-faced young man in uniform slipped from the booth and dropped to the ground.

Fatima led them around the nose of the shuttle as voices came from the shuttle's hatchway above calling to Chrisman and demanding to know what had happened. On the other side of the shuttle a tow truck was pulling to a stop and an electric car was approaching.

Mohammed spoke rapidly to Fatima in the foreign language they shared, and she responded curtly. A man in coveralls got out of the passenger side of the tow truck. "What's that lounge doing here? Has it got people in—?" The man saw Chrisman and stopped.

At the same time the electric car came to a stop behind the truck and the driver got out. "What's going on—?" He stopped.

"All you—truck driver, too," Fatima said, pressing her dagger into the soft flesh under Chrisman's chin as if to emphasize her command of the situation. "Go other side of shuttle. Stay! Do right, Chrisman not be hurt. Hostages not be hurt. Do not—be much bloodshed."

The driver of the truck got out of the far side. Chrisman said, "Do as they say. Let's get as many people out of this as we can."

Slowly the three men strung themselves out and rounded the nose of the shuttle.

"Get into car—back seat," Fatima told Johnson and the young woman. "Get in also," she told Mohammed. "Keep knife ready. Kill if move." Mohammed swallowed hard and followed them.

The young man in uniform led Chrisman to the automobile and pushed him into the passenger side of the front seat while Fatima was getting into the driver's side. "This electric car," she said. "Only steer and push to go. Right hand for knife. Mohammed has knife. You move—you die."

"Don't worry," Chrisman said calmly. "I'm not going to do anything rash, and I'm sure these others are not going to do anything either."

The young woman murmured something weakly that sounded like assent, and Johnson said, "We'll all be sensible."

Ahead of them the tow truck began to move, and the car in which the rest were riding followed as it left the runway and, picking up speed, headed toward a section of fence around the perimeter of the airport. A moment later it plunged through the fence, and the car followed through the gap, crossing the flattened chain links. In a few moments, rolling across grass, the truck and the car behind it had reached the highway. The truck stopped. The driver got out and opened the car door beside Chrisman, motioned him to move over, and got in beside him, his knife in his hand. The car rolled onto the highway, got off at the first exit, and pulled up behind a traditional automobile parked along a side street. They got into the other car and it sped off into the hills of Virginia.

The building was an old farmhouse. They reached it by a dirt road after they had been traveling in hills for half an hour. It was isolated: they had not seen another dwelling for at least fifteen minutes. The house was set in a valley and was surrounded by large trees. It would have been a pleasant place under other circumstances. The hostages did not see the inside of the house, but it looked as if it had not been occupied regularly for some time. The roof was mossy and places on it seemed damp or discolored, and the wood siding had not been painted for many years.

The hostages were led to a barn that seemed even older and in poorer repair than the house. It had been converted into a prison by first nailing shut all the doors except a small one set into the main barn door, and then nailing new planks, startling in their contrast to the weathered wood they covered, across all the openings, including the hayloft door. The hostages were led and pushed from the car to the barn and through the small door. When they were close, they could see that it had been equipped with a large new bolt.

The young woman was tense and seemed close to hysteria. Chrisman was calm and thoughtful. Johnson was quiet, as if he knew something that the others did not. Mohammed was nervous, particularly when his sister told him that he would stay with the hostages inside the makeshift prison.

"Let's talk this over," Chrisman said, turning just inside the barn, looking out through the still-open doorway at his captors. "Surely we—"

"No talk," Fatima said. "Talk for leaders. They do what we ask, you go free."

"But what do you want?"

"No talk!" she repeated fiercely.

At her tone, her uniformed companion lifted the revolver he had retrieved from the glove compartment of the car and waved it threateningly. Chrisman opened his mouth again and Johnson touched his arm cautioningly.

Fatima took the plastic knife from Mohammed's shaky hand. She said something in their foreign language. Mohammed protested, and then she spoke in English. "You no need. Guard outside. They attack, you yell. You listen! They plan something, they whisper so you not hear, you tell. We bring food soon." She pushed him gently inside and closed the door behind him.

They stood in the semidarkness of the barn's interior. The night was not yet upon them, but here in the valley only a few beams of sunshine penetrated, and only a few of those got through chinks in the barn's siding; still, it was enough to reveal them to each other and the interior of the barn. On the dirt floor a few worn blankets had been tossed on mounds of old hay. The place smelled of dirt and mold and decaying vegetation. On the left a ladder led to the hayloft. Chrisman climbed it with catlike grace, moved around in the loft, and then quietly came back down.

"Well," the young woman said, her voice close to breaking. "Is there a way out?"

Chrisman looked at Mohammed.

"You're the great scientist!" the girl said. "Surely you can find a way out for us?"

"There's a solution to every problem," Chrisman said

evenly. "But we don't want to discuss it in front of our guard here."

"He won't do anything," the girl said scornfully. "He couldn't even hijack an airplane."

"I try," Mohammed said. "But if you talk I must tell. If you go apart to talk, I must tell that, too. I not want to see harm come to you. I not want to see bad things happen. But I must do these things that I am told."

"Any solution ought to involve Mohammed," Johnson said reasonably. "It ought to be good for him, too."

"Sometimes it's impossible for everybody to win," Chrisman said.

"And sometimes if everybody doesn't win, nobody wins," Johnson said. "We've all had experience with that lately. But first maybe we should introduce ourselves. I'm Bill Johnson, and this is Mohammed."

"I gather some of you already know me," Chrisman said. "I'm Henry Chrisman."

"And you invented the bomb neutralizer among other things," the young woman said. "That almost solved the terrorist problem."

Mohammed's face brightened with understanding. "Ah, yes!"

"But not quite," Chrisman said ruefully. "And you are . . . ?"

"Jan Delaney," she said. "I'm nobody. I was going to visit my sister in Washington when all this happened. My first trip to Washington. My first trip anywhere on an airplane. And all this had to happen! I'm a computer programmer in Los Angeles . . ."

"I'm just a nobody, too," Johnson said. "But maybe if we try very hard, we can come up with an answer to this problem."

"It must have been just a great stroke of luck, picking me off like that," Chrisman mused. "They must have had their people planted at Dulles waiting for a target of opportunity, and I fell into their hands. They might have had to wait for years." His voice changed. "My wife will be worried."

"My people have learned patience," Mohammed said proudly.

"I hope they are able to learn something else," Johnson said.

"We can always kick our way out of here," Chrisman said, looking at Mohammed. "This old barn is ready to fall apart if you lean against it. But it will make noise. The question is: who will get hurt?"

"We don't want anyone to get hurt," Johnson said.

"Mr. Johnson here is not only a lover of terrorists," Delaney said scornfully, "but a coward as well."

"If anyone gets hurt," Johnson said, "it not only will be a personal tragedy, it will make the situation worse for everybody."

"The question is: What are their demands?" Chrisman said, leaning back against a pillar. The pillar creaked, and Chrisman straightened up.

"No matter what their demands are, we can't do anything about them," Johnson said. "And no matter what the official response is, it can't make anything better."

"How's that?" Chrisman asked. He spread a couple of blankets on the hay and sat down on one of them. "Sorry," he said to Delaney. "I've had a hard day."

"So have I," she said, and sat down on the other blanket, not far from him, as if casting her lot with the famous scientist. If it came to a vote, it was clear it would be two of them against one of Johnson.

"All they can ask for is something that will improve their ability to terrorize: jailed terrorists, a dismantling of security measures, money, weapons, airplanes . . ." Johnson said evenly. "They know they can't get Palestine back for us." He looked at Chrisman and smiled. "For you. We don't count."

"In this kind of thing," Chrisman said, "nobody counts. We're all pretty small in comparison to the size of the problem."

"It's that we've got to solve," Johnson said.

Delaney looked scornful. "You think you're going to solve the problem of terrorism here in this barn, in a few hours, when all the world's wisest men haven't been able to do anything about it in the last twenty-five years?"

"Maybe we've got the last good chance," Johnson said.

"If you have an idea maybe we shouldn't discuss it in front of our friend here," Chrisman said, nodding at Mohammed.

"I go back there," Mohammed said proudly, pointing toward a dark corner of the barn. The last of the beams of sunlight had disappeared, and only the darkening twilight kept the gloom from being total.

"Any solution would have to involve you," Johnson said to Mohammed.

"Some kind of solution!" Delaney said, sniffing.

"Let him talk," Chrisman said. "I like the way this man thinks." He settled back on his elbows as if to listen, but just then the door opened.

"Is all right, Mohammed?" Fatima asked from outside.

Mohammed nodded and then realizing she could not see him, said in a shaky voice, "Yes."

Another Middle Easterner, one they had not seen before, came through the door with a pistol in his hand. Behind him came Fatima with a sandwich-filled paper plate in one hand and a thermos jug in the other. "You not hunger," she said, "as so many of our people." She put the plate and the jug on the dirt floor of the barn, and motioned her head at Mohammed as she turned and went back through the doorway.

Shamefacedly avoiding the gazes of the hostages, Mohammed followed his sister through the doorway. In a few minutes he returned. The guard looked hard at him and then retreated through the door. The door closed. They could hear it bolted.

"I tell my sister nothing," Mohammed said. "I know not if she believe me."

"Hell," Delaney said, "I don't believe you."

"There was nothing to tell," Chrisman said. "Now. What's your idea?" he said to Johnson.

As if he were gauging their capacities to understand and to change, Johnson looked at the scientist sprawled back on the blanket and the young woman sitting tensely on hers, hugging her knees to her chest, and the young Palestinian standing nervously apologetic nearby. "First, perhaps we should eat before the food gets any older," he said and smiled. "And maybe we can think better when we have food in our stomachs."

Delaney didn't want to let Mohammed have any of the sandwiches until Chrisman commented wryly, between bites of the dry bread and cheese, that the food might be poisoned, and then she wouldn't eat until she had seen the effect on Mohammed, even after Chrisman apologized and pointed out that it wouldn't make sense to poison them when they could be disposed of just as easily in other ways, and in any case they wouldn't take the chance of poisoning one of their own. But Delaney's fears were not logical. Finally, however, they had all eaten and drunk the cool, iceless, odd-tasting water, though Delaney had spit out a mouthful when Chrisman said, "Of course the water may be drugged to put us out—I'm sorry. It's just water from an old well."

By now they were all seated on blankets, and the barn was almost completely dark. Their captors had not provided a light, and they were faceless voices in the dark, like children telling ghost stories late at night. "Of course we could break out of here now," Chrisman said quietly. "It's hard to believe they have enough guards to catch us in the darkness. Of course, we would have to blunder around among the trees and brush. They might have automatic weapons, and one of the terrorists might lose his head and open fire. We wouldn't know what direction to go, either. We couldn't go back down the dirt road or we'd be recaptured for sure. There'll be a full moon later tonight. That would help us, but it would help them, too. And there's our friend, here."

"What would you do?" Johnson asked.

"I—I . . ." Mohammed said, as if unable to answer.

"That's something," Johnson said.

"Of course if we decide to break out, we've got to do it in the next hour or so, while it's still dark," Chrisman said.

"I've got to go to the bathroom," Delaney said suddenly. "I can't hold it any longer."

"It's dark," Chrisman said, "and there are lots of corners."

"There also may be rats and spiders," she said.

"And snakes," Chrisman said. He seemed to take pleasure in teasing her.

"Maybe I can wait," she said.

"We have an hour," Johnson said. "We should give them time to get bored and sleepy, anyway. We can talk."

"Let's talk," Chrisman said.

"We're fortunate in a way," Johnson said. "We have a representative group: a reluctant terrorist, someone who is terrified, and a couple of reasonable people, one of whom is in a position to recommend a solution that might be considered seriously by the authorities."

"Aren't we lucky," Delaney said. Her small attempt at sarcasm was undercut by the break in her voice.

"Yes," Johnson said.

"What's your idea, Johnson?" Chrisman said lazily.

"Most of the problems with terrorism seem to be involved with the ownership of land," Johnson said. "Particularly homelands. And particularly when a piece of land is homeland to more than one people."

"Religion also seems to play a part," Chrisman said.

"Yes, but usually when it is associated with some kind of nationalistic movement. The big problem seems to be land."

"And, as Will Rogers once said," Chrisman said, "they ain't making any more."

"That's the point," Johnson said. "If I'm right, we have almost reached the stage where we can make more."

Chrisman sat up in the darkness, the hay making an audible squeak under the blanket. "Yeah."

"That's the work you're involved in, I believe," Johnson said. "You're not a regular astronaut. This sort of thing is what took you into space."

"Making land," Chrisman said. "It might work."

"I don't understand what you two are talking about!" Delaney protested.

"Me also," Mohammed said helplessly.

"Space habitats," Chrisman said. "That's what I'm into. Making places in space where people can live. Out of materials constructed on Earth and transported into space to be put together there for living quarters, laboratories, factories. At first, anyway. Later getting raw materials from the moon. Much later moving large asteroids into orbit around the Earth, mining them for iron and other minerals, hollowing them into habitats, maybe mobile ones containing their own gravity, air, air-renewal system, farms, factories, propulsion systems. Eventually making them self-sufficient, maybe capable of carrying the inhabitants anywhere they want to go in the solar system, maybe anywhere in the galaxy."

His enthusiasm was evident, even in the darkness. It was clear that he had thought about this a great deal and even made speeches about it.

"I don't see what good that's going to do us," Delaney said. "I wouldn't live in a place like that, even if we get out of here alive."

"Nobody's asking you to, Delaney," Chrisman said. "We're going to ask Mohammed here."

"Me?" Mohammed said. In the darkness his expression could only be imagined.

"How would you like to live in a world orbiting the Earth?" Chrisman said.

"I be frightened," Mohammed said. "How I live? How I breathe?"

"Those things would be taken care of," Chrisman said. "You would be taught things. And there would be others there. Your sister. The rest of your people eventually. Anybody who wants to go."

"There be millions," Mohammed said. "You put all in space?"

"Those who want to go. The committed. The terrorists. The adventurous. Some will refuse. But think: the Palestinians protest because they say they have been cheated of their heritage and their future. If they go to live in space habitats, the future will be theirs."

"Theirs only?"

"Of course there will be others," Chrisman said. "Other dissident groups to begin with, but once it gets rolling young people of many nationalities will want their own chance in space."

"My people not know such things as space—what you say—habitats."

"The Palestinians are intelligent and well-educated, and anybody who can handle explosives secretly without blowing themselves up can learn how to take the necessary precautions to live in space. It requires forethought, but this is something your people are good at. The Irish? Maybe they can learn."

"You mean we would go to the great expense of putting these living quarters into space so that terrorists could live in them?" Delaney said incredulously.

"That's the beauty of it, don't you see?" Chrisman said. "Humanity's future lies in space. It doesn't matter who goes first. It's all of us. Right now there aren't enough people who can see this clearly enough to finance it. But maybe we can get enough support by making it serve two purposes: we'll solve the terrorist problem and get the space habitats started at the same time."

"But that's rewarding the terrorists for killing people," Delaney protested.

"We can't afford that kind of thinking," Johnson said.

"It's just solving the problem," Chrisman said impatiently. He seemed to have adopted the idea as if it were his own. "You don't realize how much money and resources go into the business of coping with terrorism. And how close terrorism might come to destroying us all in a nuclear war if the wrong people get their hands on nuclear weapons, or somebody miscalculates. We could lose everything."

"Maybe my people not go," Mohammed said. "This space thing not be Palestine."

"There are many reasons why your people should accept a generous offer. Not the least is their pride. It would be dangerous. Some would die in accidents. There would be martyrs. But there would be peace, and a land brighter and richer than Palestine."

"Then the Jews would want one," Delaney said.

"Let them have one," Chrisman said. "Let anybody who wants a habitat have one if they can afford it or the funds can be raised somewhere. People will be too busy in space making things work to worry about old antagonisms. Just like the settlers were too busy in America. Maybe, if we all work at it, we can turn our competitive instincts toward our galactic environment rather than each other."

"There still will be problems," Johnson said.

"Oh, of course," Chrisman said. "This isn't utopia. It just gives us breathing room. And maybe it scatters humanity's seed far enough that a single accident can't wipe it out. If we can just get it done, it will mean that humanity is immortal. Or at least as immortal as the universe."

"Maybe it work," Mohammed said. For the first time he sounded hopeful.

"You think your sister would go for it?" Delaney said. For the first time she sounded hopeful, too.

"Maybe." He seemed excited now. He moved toward the door, stumbling in the darkness, and pounded on it.

The noise was startling in the night. A voice outside spoke loud, harsh words in a foreign language, and Mohammed replied in the same language. The captives could make out the word "Fatima." It was repeated several times.

"Already?" Chrisman said. "At this time of night?"

"Why not?" Delaney said. She was standing. "Johnson? Are you there?"

"Yes." Johnson felt a hand touch his and cling to it for a moment.

"I'm sorry," she said. She released his hand. It was enough. She, too, had the capacity to change. She laughed. "I'm going to the bathroom while I have the chance."

The door opened. Through the doorway came the light of the full moon outlining the figure of Mohammed's sister and casting a long shaft of silver across the barn floor.

"Fatima," Mohammed said confidently, "I have good idea. . . ."

The prisoners were released on a street corner in Washington, D.C., not far from a telephone booth and only half a dozen blocks from Capitol Hill. Mohammed had been persuasive, but inbred paranoia was not quickly discarded. There was much work to be done; it would take time, years perhaps.

"Do you think it will work, Johnson?" Chrisman asked as he waited for Delaney to be finished with the telephone.

"I know it will," Johnson said. His eyes had the look of someone who was seeing distant visions.

"You have people here?" Chrisman asked. "You need a lift somewhere?"

"Don't worry about me," Johnson said. "But do you have a piece of paper on you?"

Chrisman looked down at his astronaut's coveralls and

CRISIS! 153

smiled. "I'm afraid not. As a matter of fact, I was going to borrow a quarter from you or Delaney for the telephone call."

Johnson rummaged through his pockets and came up with a quarter. "Here," he said, and when Chrisman turned to the telephone booth, he walked quickly away.

In an alley between office buildings he found an area enclosed by overflowing trash containers and large cardboard boxes. He rummaged through the containers until he found a small box, tore the flap from it, settled down behind one of the large ones, and held the flap up to a distant streetlight as he wrote:

"Your name is Bill Johnson. You have just helped solve the problem of political terrorism and launched humanity toward the stars, and you don't remember. You may find the newspapers filled with reports of what happened, but you will find no mention of the part you played.

"For this there are several possible explanations. . . ."

After he had finished, he propped the flap against an adjacent trash container where he would see it when he awoke, pulled his jacket tightly around him against the night's chill, and lay back to await the new day.

Episode Five
Woman of the Year

The man lying behind the large cardboard boxes and the overflowing trash containers opened his eyes to a half-circle of faces framed against the blue sky. One of the faces was older and sterner. Below it was a blue uniform. "You can't sleep here, mister," it said.

The man pulled his old gray tweed jacket a little tighter around his body and sat up. "I wasn't doing much sleeping, I assure you," he said and grinned.

It was a good grin and a pleasant face, even though it seemed a bit blank at the moment as if it had been wiped clean by the night's healing hand. The face was a golden brown, not as if it had been tanned but as if that was its native color, and it was smooth as if fresh shaven, although clearly the man had not had the opportunity to shave. He had dark, curly hair, and when he got up, as he did now, he was of medium height. In fact, though he may have been better looking than most, he seemed an average sort of person, a man easily overlooked by those who only passed by.

"We don't allow vagrants around here," the policeman said. "The Capitol and the White House ain't that far away. It don't look good."

The policeman was surrounded by children, big and little, white and black and brown, clean and dirty, neat and ragged. They had gathered as if by magic to stare at this curiosity in their midst. By their dress and the books in their hands, some of them were on their way to school. Others, perhaps, were only loitering, looking for excitement or trouble. One of the younger children stuck her tongue out. The man smiled at her. An older boy dressed in ragged jeans and a dirty jacket held his right hand with the thumb hooked over his waistband near his back pocket as if it held an amulet, and his eyes were narrow and calculating as he studied the man who had been sleeping in this dirty alley. "Whatcha doin' here anyway?" he asked.

The man patted his pockets and pulled a billfold out of the rear one. He opened it for the policeman's inspection. "I've got money and credit cards," he said. There were a few bills in it and a couple of plastic cards. "I just got trapped here last night and couldn't get a cab, so I decided to wait out the night. Pretty cold, too."

"Okay, what's your name?" the policeman asked, taking out a pad of paper and a pencil.

The man looked at one of the cards. "Bill Johnson," he said.

"You don't know your own name?"

"Just a habit, officer," the man said. "I'd rather you didn't write this up, however. After all, I haven't broken any laws."

"You think sleeping in the street is legal in this town?" the policeman asked.

"I think he's a looney," the older boy said. He was looking at the billfold in Johnson's hand.

"Go on about your business, Tommy, if you have any," the policeman said.

"What's going on here, officer?" asked a woman's voice from behind the throng of children.

The policeman turned, motioning to the children as if he were parting the Red Sea. "Get away. Go along to school or wherever you're headed. It's just this man here, Ms. Franklin," he said to the young woman unveiled by the children. "I found him sleeping behind these boxes, and I'm trying to find out what's going on."

"Is everything all right?" the woman named Franklin asked. She was of medium height and slender, with dark blonde hair and blue eyes and a face and figure of unusual beauty. The younger children clustered around her and the older boys gave her room, appraising her out of the corner of their eyes and unconsciously straightening their backs and brushing the hair from their eyes.

"Perfectly fine, ma'am," Johnson said. He smiled at her.

"Says his name's Johnson, Bill Johnson," the policeman said, putting away his pad and pencil.

"I'll be responsible for Mr. Johnson," the woman said. "I'll see that he gets wherever he's going."

"That's fine with me, Ms. Franklin," the policeman said. "Get along to school, you kids! Go on, now!"

The children stirred but did not disperse. The policeman moved off unhappily, as if searching for more satisfying situations.

"Do you want to come with me?" the woman said.

"Very much," Johnson said.

"You can go on about your own business if you like," she continued. "I'm going to work, but I can find you a taxicab or a hotel." Her voice was lovely, too, low and melodious.

"You're kind," Johnson said.

She shrugged. "Just common courtesy."

"I was hoping for more." He dusted himself off and straightened his clothing. "I'm ready."

They moved out of the alley onto the street, the children following them as if one of them were the Pied Piper. "So your name is Bill Johnson," she said.

"I think so," he said.

They were halfway down the street when Johnson stopped suddenly. "Can you wait just a moment?" he asked. "I've forgotten something." He turned and ran back the way they had come, and down the odorous alley to the spot where he had been lying. He looked around the area for a moment and saw a piece of cardboard with some writing on it. He glanced at it, folded it so that the writing was inside, and walked quickly back toward the little group with the piece of cardboard in his hand. The children were clustered around the young woman. It was clear now who was the Pied Piper. Johnson studied her as she talked to the children, clearly caring about them.

"Okay," he said.

She looked up at him and smiled. "Go on to school, children," she said. For her they did what they would not do for the man in uniform, moving off, chattering and waving their hands. "I'm Sally Franklin," she said. "And I work in the People, Limited, building just down the street. If you want to walk there with me, we can get you settled somewhere. Where is it you belong?"

"Would you believe me if I told you I don't know?" he asked.

She tilted her head to look at him as they walked along. "I'm in the business of believing people."

"You're good at it," Johnson said. "That's because you like people, and they like you." He looked at her as if he were seeing not only the person in front of him but all the people she had been and might yet become.

Within a couple of blocks, the streets were busier, the sidewalks were cleaner, and the buildings were large and institutional, with sawed-limestone exteriors and polished brass street markers on their corners. Where there were brief stretches of green lawn in front of or beside the buildings, some of them had neat signs identifying them. One of them read "People, Limited."

"This is where I work," she said, turning in at the doorway. She had her purse open in her hand and an identification card inserted in a slot beside the plate-glass doors. They swung open and she motioned Johnson to go in.

An attractive dark-haired young woman seated at a desk just inside the doorway looked up as they entered. "Good morning, Ms. Franklin," she said and gave a curious look at Johnson, but didn't say anything, as if she were accustomed to seeing the other woman with strange companions.

"Jessie, this is Mr. Johnson," Sally Franklin said. "I found him in an alley." She smiled at Johnson as if to say it was a joke between them. "See if you can find him a place to stay, or transportation, or whatever he needs."

"How about a job?" Johnson said.

"You don't have a job?" Franklin asked.

"I don't think so."

"There's a great deal you don't know about yourself," she said, looking at him without accusation, "but that's none of my business. We're always looking for volunteers. We don't have many paid positions, but why don't you fill out an application, listing your qualifications and employment record, if you have any, and if we can't find something for you here maybe we can locate employment elsewhere."

"You really are kind," he said, holding out his hand.

She took his hand and pressed it briefly. "I seem to get involved with people who don't have a home or a future," she said and smiled. She turned toward the elevator a few feet away.

"Strays?" he asked.

"Strays," she agreed.

"Thanks for everything," he said.

She stepped into the elevator with a wave of her hand and was gone. "She's a remarkable woman," Johnson said, turning to the young woman at the desk.

"Without her this organization would be nothing," she said.

"What's her position with this organization?" Johnson asked.

"She *is* the organization. Executive director," the woman said shortly as if impatient with Johnson's presence.

"She's very young to have such a responsibility. And very beautiful."

"What's wrong with that?" the woman at the desk asked sharply. "She's very smart, too."

"I can see that," Johnson said. "It's just that from her appearance and her way with children, she looks as if she should be adding to the population, not trying to reduce it."

"That's all you men think about," the woman said, biting off her words. "Well, she's got more important ambitions, and you ought to be thankful she has. Overpopulation is the most important problem of our time." Clearly the subject was the focus of her life, and she was just getting warmed up to it.

Johnson held up his hands in submission. "I'm a convert," he said.

"People take advantage of Sally," the woman said, almost as if to herself. There was no doubt that she included Johnson in that group. "Someday, unless there's some providence watching over her, she's going to have a bad experience—and then I'm afraid of what will happen."

"Yes," Johnson said. He paused and added, "I'd like to help. I'd like to look after her."

"You?" the woman asked skeptically.

"I may not seem impressive at the moment," Johnson said, "but I do feel a sense of commitment to what this woman is doing. It's terribly important. And I feel as if there is some danger to her and to what she is doing that I might be able to help with. I would work cheap—for nothing, if I could live on it."

The woman looked at him as if she was impressed in spite of herself. "Do you want that application?" she asked.

"How about the place to stay first—not too far away, perhaps, and not too expensive."

A few minutes and a few telephone calls later, Johnson was back on the sidewalk with an address and directions on a slip of paper in his pocket. He still had the piece of cardboard in his hand. He paused at the first corner to unfold it and read:

"Your name is Bill Johnson. You have just helped solve the problem of political terrorism and launched humanity toward the stars, and you don't remember. You may find the newspapers filled with reports of what happened, but you will find no mention of the part you played.

"For this there are several possible explanations, including the likelihood that I may be lying or deceived or insane. But the explanation on which you must act is that I have told you the truth: you are a man who was born in a future that has almost used up all hope; you were sent to this time and place to alter the events that created that future.

"Am I telling the truth? The only evidence you have is your apparently unique ability to foresee consequences—it comes like a vision, not of the future because the future can be changed, but of what will happen if events take their natural course, if someone does not act, if you do not intervene.

"But each time you intervene, no matter how subtly, you change the future from which you came. You exist in this time and outside of time and in the future, and so each change makes you forget.

"I wrote this message last night to tell you what I know, just as I learned about myself this morning by reading a message printed in lipstick on a bathroom mirror, for I am you and we are one, and we have done this many times before."

The man named Bill Johnson stared unseeing down the long street until he stirred himself, tore the piece of cardboard into pieces, and stuffed them into a trash receptacle. When he looked up he saw the older boy in the jeans and dirty jacket. He still had his thumb hooked over his waistband. But he wasn't watching Johnson. He was watching the front door of People, Limited.

The hotel was half a dozen blocks away, on the uneasy edge between the White-House–Mall–Capitol-Hill area of massive stone government buildings and the decaying slums teeming with children and crime and poverty that half encircled it. The edge was continually shifting, like an uncertain battlefield between armies of ancient antagonists, as old areas deteriorated into near-abandonment or were torn down to make way for big new structures, some of them commemorating the dead and gone, some of them dedicated to a dream of things to come.

The battle for the soul of the hotel was still in doubt, but the dusty lobby, presided over by an elderly clerk all alone in what had once been bustle and glitter, was haunted by a premonition of defeat. The room to which Johnson admitted himself was a little cleaner, but it too had the kind of embedded dirt and irrepressible odors that nothing but total renewal could ever obliterate. It held an old bed, a couple of tattered understuffed chairs, a floor lamp, a telephone and a table lamp on a nightstand beside the bed, and a bathroom with pitted porcelain tub, cracked lavatory, and stained toilet, a single towel but no washcloth, and a hand-sized bar of Ivory soap that crackled with age when Johnson unwrapped it.

The one new object in the room was a color television set, some owner's forlorn attempt at remodeling. Johnson stared at it for a moment when he came out of the bathroom and turned it on. A soap opera titled "All My Children" swam into view. Johnson ignored it and began to go through his pockets. The billfold that he already had glanced at was remarkably bare of identification other than a Visa card and a social security card enclosed in plastic; he also had a few coins, a few bills, some of them oddly colored and labeled "King Scrip," which he crumpled and threw in the wastebasket, a pocket comb, and the receipt for a one-way airline ticket from Los Angeles to Washington, D.C., arriving at Dulles Airport. It had a baggage claim check stapled to it.

Johnson looked up the telephone number for the airline, dialed it, and asked the disinterested clerk if she could have his bag delivered to him at the hotel. At first she refused to do it, but when he insisted he didn't have transportation, something must have clicked in her memory, for she suddenly asked if he had been on the plane whose mobile lounge had been hijacked.

"All I want is my bag," he said. "I don't have any clothes."

"But if you were—"

"It doesn't matter," he said. "Do me a favor. Mark it up to public relations. I'll leave the claim check with the desk clerk in case I'm not here."

When he turned back to the television set, the soap opera was over. A commercial had already started. It showed vast numbers of children covering all the curved surface of what seemed to be part of a globe. They were all races, all colors, well-dressed and ragged, but many of them looked hungry and misshapen and sad. They were all moving toward the viewer, and as they got closer and bigger, more of them kept coming behind, and there was no end to them and they blotted out the screen.

In the darkness that followed, a woman's voice said, "Children are a blessing and a joy. But not when there are more of them than a family can feed and care for and love. Then they are a reproach and a tragedy and a sin. And the human family has been having too many of them recently." The screen cleared and revealed Sally Franklin dressed in a neat, pale-blue suit standing in front of a full-color reproduction of the Earth as seen from space. "World population was two and a half billion in 1950, three and two-thirds billion in 1970, nearly four and a half billion in 1980." The view of Earth that had been bright with sunshine, streaks of clouds, and blue seas steadily darkened. "The end is in sight. And the answer is up to you, every one of you. Before you create more babies—think! Think about not only whether you can care for them, but whether this world of ours has room for them. It's better to have one or two happy children than three or four that don't have enough, better to have two billion people on Earth with a chance for the future than eight billion or eighteen billion with no chance at all. It's our decision. All of us. It is not the problem of people who live somewhere else whose skin is a different color or who belong to a different race. It's our problem. All of us. And we've got to solve it. All of us. Or else. . . ." The circle of the Earth had turned completely black and so, with startling suddenness, did the entire television screen. With equal suddenness, white words sprang out upon the screen that read "People, Limited," and a man's voice said, "The preceding message was brought to you by this network as a public service. It is being shown, in appropriate translations, in every part of the world reached by television, and elsewhere by film or other means."

Johnson reached over and turned off the television set, picked up his jacket, and left the room.

The receptionist at People, Limited, looked up from the employment form and said, "What can I do with this? Outside of your name, there's no information on it."

Johnson smiled. "If I were trying to deceive anybody, I would have made up something. It's just that I have a problem with my memory. If I have a past, I don't remember it. If I have a work record, I don't know what it is. If I have an education, I don't know where. If I have skills, I don't know what they are." Before she could speak, he went on, "But I do have a commitment to what this organization and Ms. Franklin are doing. And I would do anything honorable to help them succeed."

She frowned and then sighed. "But what can I do? Our personnel people will just throw this out."

"I'll work as a volunteer," Johnson said. "Anything that would let me watch over Ms. Franklin."

Neat and unthreatening, he stood in front of the reception desk in the polished, well-lighted lobby, looking directly into the eyes of the dark-haired receptionist.

"How would you live?" she asked.

"That's not important."

She sighed again. "I'll put you on the temporary employment list. The personnel people don't have to approve that for a week. Maybe by that time you'll have proven yourself of some value."

"Oh, I will," Johnson said.

"It only pays minimum wage. Just turn in your hours to me at the end of the day. . . ."

"Don't worry," he said. "My goals are the same as yours."

"I hope so," she said.

The elevator doors opened, and Sally Franklin came out followed by a man and a woman talking rapidly to her. She had an attache case in her hand, and she was listening and responding in fragments when she saw Johnson. She stopped. "You're still here?" she said.

"I'm back," he said. "To be your bodyguard, your personal assistant, your porter, your gopher...."

Franklin looked sharply at the receptionist. "But I don't need anybody like that."

The receptionist looked embarrassed and helpless. "He—I...."

Johnson shrugged and spread his hands. "It seems I'm not good for anything else."

Franklin looked at him and shook her head. "Oh, all right. But we've got to find something else for you to do." She turned to the other two. "I think I've got it all. Johnson will go with me to the press conference. You can stay here and work on the Delhi meeting."

Outside, Johnson reached for Franklin's attache case, and after a brief resistance she let it go. "It gives me something to do," he said.

"Oh, all right. It isn't far. But I don't know what I'm going to do with you."

"Nothing," Johnson said. "Nothing at all. You won't even know I'm around."

"What brought you here?" she asked.

"I don't know," he said. "I only know what I'm doing here."

"And what is that?"

"Trying to protect you—and what you're trying to do."

She shook her head. "What makes you think you can do that?"

He laughed. "Do you want me to list my qualifications?"

They were walking east on the broad avenue and Franklin kept glancing sideways at Johnson as if trying to understand him. "I usually have a feeling about people," she said, "but I can't get a handle on you. You're going to have to tell me something about yourself—all these mysterious statements about not knowing where you belong or if you have a job or what brought you here. That was all right as long as you were a . . ."

"A stray?" Johnson suggested.

"Yes. But if you're going to be—"

"Your faithful servant?"

"—I need to know more about you." She finished breathlessly. "Why do you make me feel so frustrated?"

"It's because I have a queer memory. It works only one way."

"It's the same with everybody."

"Mine works forward, not back." He hesitated for the first time. "I'd rather not tell you any more. It will make you sorry for me, and I don't want that. The result—"

"Hang the result," she said, almost angrily. "You can't stop now."

"I remember the future," he said. "But I don't remember the past. I seem to wake up periodically without any personal memories, but I have glimpses of what the future might be like."

She gave him a sidelong glance. "That must be—disturbing."

"I know it's hard to believe, and I'm not asking you to believe it. Only to believe that I hope to do good and that I would never do you harm."

"Can you see my future?" she asked.

"Are you teasing me?"

"Can't you tell? No, that's unfair. I'm trying not to."

"I'd rather not tell you. Believe me, it's a burden."

"Tell me," she commanded. "What's in my future?"

"I see only flashes," he said reluctantly. "That's the

way it always comes—a vision, not of the future because there are many futures, but of the natural consequence of any set of circumstances. And it shifts, like the image in a kaleidoscope, from moment to moment, as individual actions and decisions reshape it. One can't look at it steadily without getting dizzy."

"You can turn it off then?" She spoke as if she was beginning to believe him.

"Only partly. Like not looking at something. You know it's there, but only as a background."

"You haven't told me my future," she reminded him.

"Some people are more important to the future than others—not more important as people but more important in that their actions and choices have more influence in shaping the future. I sense them as a kind of nexus, a place where lines to the future converge and make the individual and the area immediately surrounding the individual more vivid, more colorful, more—real."

"And that attracts you?"

"Like a moth to the flame," he said and smiled. "The serious answer is: Sometimes."

"What decides?"

"The future," Johnson said simply. "Sometimes I can't stand to look at it, and then I have to do something."

"To make it better?"

"To help others make it better. I'm speaking theoretically, of course, because I can't remember what has happened before—if it *has* happened before, and I am not just living a great delusion. But I can't perceive the consequences of my own actions except as they are related to someone else. It's as if I had a blind spot, like being able to see everybody but yourself. So I can't know what would happen if I did something. Only if someone else does something."

"You still haven't told me anything about myself."

"You're starting to believe me."

"Shouldn't I?"

"You see the consequences in me."

"You're not so bad. You're thoughtful, gentle, kind. . . ."

"Troubled, sad, distant. . . ." He smiled. "You see? I said that one of us would end up feeling sorry for me."

"You said I would, and you're right. You haven't told me in so many words, but apparently you see me as one of those persons you were talking about."

"Do you really want to know how important you are?"

She thought about it. "I guess not," she said and smiled in a way that seemed to brighten the air around her. "Besides, we're here."

"Here" was the side entrance to a large public building. They went through the doorway and through a backstage area to the wings of a small auditorium. A harried, balding little man was waiting for them. "Sally," he said, "they're waiting for you. This is a tough bunch, and they're getting tougher. I've been listening. I think they're going to give you a hard time."

Franklin patted him on the shoulder and winked. "Don't worry, Fred. It does them good to wait for a few minutes. And I'm not worried about a few cynical reporters." She turned to Johnson and retrieved her attache case. "How am I going to do?" she asked softly.

"Great," Johnson said.

She smiled at him and walked to the center of the stage where a wooden lectern, so massive it looked as if it had been built into the hall, had been placed. Although the auditorium was small, the audience filled only the first few rows. The overhead lights were pitiless. Franklin looked lost behind the lectern as she opened her attache case and removed a handful of papers, though she never afterward referred to them, and stood for a moment looking out at the puddle of skeptical faces. "I'm Sally Franklin, executive director of People, Limited, and I've been asked to make myself available for questions about our new program for population control. By 'our' I mean not only People, Limited, but Zero Population Growth, Planned Parenthood, and half a dozen other groups dedicated to the problem of overpopulation. Each of our organizations has its own program, but we are coordinating our educational efforts for this drive.

"The year coming up has been designated the International Population Year. Every cooperating nation will be conducting a census that is expected to be more accurate than anything presently available. Each one also will gather data on population growth, resources, and resource projections. All of this information will be placed in databanks for further study and reference. The mission assigned to People, Limited, and other privately supported groups concerned with overpopulation is to educate people to the need and means for family planning. We have prepared extensive campaigns, for which the commercials on television that you may have been seeing lately are the first contributions by People, Limited. We are preparing others, including what we call a 'Pop Quiz.' Are there questions? The gentleman in the first row."

The man who stood up was lean, dark, and gloomy. He bit off his words as if they were bullets. "Ray Minor, UPI. You refer to these programs as educational, which implies that there is general agreement about the facts of the situation. I have two questions about this: first, isn't this, in fact, propaganda for a particular viewpoint; and second, what do you propose to do about groups, particularly religious groups, that believe there is no overpopulation problem or that to practice contraception is a sin?"

Franklin smiled sweetly at the reporter. "You always ask difficult questions, Mr. Minor. It is true that one person's education is another person's propaganda, but we have facts to back our beliefs. The proper course of action to deal with the facts always is an appropriate subject for discussion, but until those who oppose measures to limit population can come up with reliable data that contradict our facts, or at least prove that our data are inaccurate, we are justified in calling our programs educational. The answer to your second question is that we must discuss these matters with religious groups as well as the general public. Morality that produces more misery in the world is inaccurately named. In any case, real opposition is not to our goals but to means, and we are not committed to any means."

A plump woman stood up in the front row. "Does that include the Pope?"

"Of course. Though personal discussion is not necessarily the way to go about it. And we do not mean to suggest that the Pope or the Church need education, only that there is room for discussion. I can announce, however, that the Vatican is considering the appointment of a study group."

A tall, older woman with graying hair stood up toward the back. "Wilma Blanchard, *Science Review*. Do you envision or see the need for technological breakthroughs?"

"New technology is always welcome. The perfection of a male contraceptive pill, for instance. But we can't wait for it. We have the technology. All we need is the will."

A broad-shouldered blond man stood up in the third

row. "Bruce Campbell, CBS. What is the problem, then, and how do you hope to deal with it?"

"The Bible commanded us to be fruitful, and multiply, and replenish the earth, and subdue it. Whether you believe in the truth of the Bible or Darwin or both, there was a long period in human existence when our survival as a species or as tribes or as families depended on a high rate of reproduction. The instincts that served us so well for so long betray us when the earth has been replenished and subdued. Science has lowered the death rate and given us the means to lower the birth rate. As long ago as the 1960s a National Academy of Sciences report concluded by saying that 'either the birth rate of the world must come down, or the death rate must go back up.' How do we deal with it? There aren't any easy solutions; in fact, the only solution is individual choice to do not what is instinctive but what is rational. And that means education."

The same plump woman in the front row spoke up again. "Doesn't that mean that the problem is insoluble?"

Franklin looked sober. "It means that the solution is difficult. Any time we must persuade the majority of the human race to be rational, we must expect difficulties, discouragement, disappointment, and defeat. But we can't give up simply because it is difficult, because giving up is death."

The woman went on as if she had not been listening, "Does what you have said mean that you disapprove of the Indian solution of compulsory sterilization and the Chinese solution of surveillance and social pressure?"

"Different cultures may require different approaches," Franklin said. "I'm not sure that compulsory sterilization ever was an official policy in India, and if it were I'm not sure that it or what you call the Chinese solution provide any final answers. I know they wouldn't work in this country or in most countries with a tradition of individual freedom, and I'm pretty sure that the only answer in the long term is individual responsibility. How one provides the individual with the information necessary to reach a responsible decision, and the means to implement it, may differ from culture to culture, but unless the necessity of limiting our family size is accepted as a truth in every culture then no solution will work. Repression ultimately breaks down, and social repression of basic instincts can only lead to the destruction of the society that represses them."

A short pudgy man in the fifth row stood up. "Harry Hopper, Associated Press. Isn't it true that overpopulation is primarily a problem of the developing countries, and, if so, aren't your missionary efforts wasted on people who already are converted, so to speak?"

"In terms of population control, you are correct. The developed countries already have reached the goal of zero population growth or dropped below it. Some Scandinavian countries have expressed concern about the fact that their reproduction rate has dropped so far that their nations may be in danger of extinction. It is a fact that the only places where population has been effectively controlled have been in industrialized nations with high standards of living, and some observers have speculated that the only way to achieve a decline in population growth is by raising the standard of living to the point where everyone recognizes that the large family, useful in an agrarian society, is an economic handicap in one that is industrialized. Raising the standard of living worldwide is a desirable goal in itself, but we believe that while efforts must continue to do so we cannot wait for that to produce the desired effect."

CRISIS!

A group of reporters were on their feet asking for the floor, but Franklin silenced them with a raised hand. "Of course, population control is only one side of the problem. The other side is resources. In the presence of unlimited resources, there can be no overpopulation, and the unfortunate fact is that the developed nations, and particularly this country, consume far more of the world's resources, per capita, than the developing countries. In fact, it has been estimated that an American baby has several hundred times the impact on the environment and the world's resources as one born in India or China. We must not only limit our numbers, we must learn to live less wastefully, to use resources more efficiently, and we must find or develop new resources and nonpolluting ways to use them."

The plump woman in the front row shouted above the others, "Are you going to take this message to the developing nations? And how will they accept it from a wealthy American?"

"It will be communicated everywhere by local leaders in their own way, with whatever help we can give them."

"What is the source of your financial support?" someone shouted.

"Contributions, large and small," Franklin said. "Our brief financial statement is available as a handout at the end of this conference. Anyone who wishes to check our books is welcome at any time at the People, Limited, headquarters."

"Are you married? Do you have children?"

"The answer to both is no. My biography is available at the headquarters as well. I can't promise that the answer to those personal questions will always be no, but if the time ever comes when I can't in good conscience continue this struggle, I will step aside and let someone else take over.

But my personal apostasy or keeping of the faith is immaterial. Humanity is what matters: if we cannot control our numbers, our numbers will control us. I think we've reached the end of this session. Thank you for your attention and your thoughtful questions. The world will appreciate your help in solving the single greatest problem of our time."

The audience stood and applauded as she picked up her papers and her attache case and left the stage.

Outside the building Franklin handed Johnson the attaché case and asked, "How did it go?"

"I was right," Johnson said. "You were great."

She blushed, though it was clear from her tone that she had expected it. "It did go well, didn't it."

"Superbly. Nobody else could have done it as well."

"Aw, shucks," she said and laughed. It was afternoon, the day was warm, the sun was shining, and it was clear that she felt relieved and happy, and that Johnson's presence somehow made it better.

The afternoon that followed was ordinary in its details but unusual in the way they responded to it. She had several potential contributors to call upon, and they traversed the streets of downtown Washington, entering doorways, ascending elevators, waiting in reception rooms, requesting grants and gifts from philanthropists and corporate directors. Sally Franklin was good at it. She presented her requests simply and without apologies, as if she were doing the donors a favor by accepting their contributions, and, in addition, on this particular day, there was beneath her efficient and serious presentation a kind of suppressed merriment that produced an unusually generous response.

Johnson spent his time listening, though his presence did nothing to diminish Franklin's effect on her contacts. They seemed to observe the way he listened and their

CRISIS!

attention was heightened. And there was talk between the two of them, although it was mostly Franklin's talk and Johnson's listening. He was a good listener, his attention all on her, perhaps because he had no distractions, no concerns of his own, no memories to interfere with the importance of the moment.

She told him about her childhood in Minneapolis, her parents, her school days, her boyfriends, and the glorious moment when a population expert came to lecture at the University and described a future that changed her life. It was reinforced a few months later when she spent a summer in crowded, overpopulated Mexico City and then, after graduation a year later, worked in social welfare in the slums of Washington. It was then she knew what her life work would be. "Poverty would not be so bad," she said, "if it did not include children. A child without food or shelter or love, without opportunity, without hope, is enough to break the heart of the world."

Johnson's look said that it broke his heart.

"This has been the best day of my life," she said exuberantly. "I think I owe it to you."

"That's nonsense," he said. "You've done it all."

"I must leave for India tonight. My bags are packed; Jessie will see that they get to the airport. I'm too excited to go home and sit. Let's have dinner. I'd like to spend a few more hours with you before we have to part. After all," she laughed, "with your history I might not see you again."

He did not look into her eyes. "Of course," he said.

They ate paella and drank sangria at a Spanish restaurant in an old house located not far from Capitol Hill but in an area of older homes, narrow, set close together, and now infecting each other with the disease of poverty and the stench of decay. Diners were scattered through a number of rooms, small and large, and singers with guitars and dancers with castanets and iron heels wandered through the rooms entertaining. Mostly Franklin and Johnson ignored everyone else; when they could not hear each other they waited, and when they could she continued to talk to him as if they were alone, to describe her plans, to ask for his advice and his vision of the future. "This isn't a gypsy tearoom," she said merrily, "and I have no tea leaves for you to read, but perhaps we can pretend...." It was clear that pretending, that getting away from the pressures of the real world, was important to her tonight.

"You will do all the things that you have planned," he said, "if you are careful."

"Careful?"

"Many things can deflect a person from accomplishment. Things can happen to change the kind of person they are or their understanding of the kind of world they live in. Or what seemed completely clear can become hazy and muddled when alternatives appear. Do you want to tell me why you've never married?"

"I've had a few opportunities," she said.

"I can believe that."

"But when I was young I didn't love any of them," she said thoughtfully, "or not enough. And since then I haven't loved any of them as much as I loved what I'm doing." She looked up at him. "Are you telling me that marriage might change me?"

"What do you think?"

"As long as I don't have children," she began and stopped. "You're saying that if I loved somebody enough to marry him I'd want to have his children. Surely that wouldn't be fatal."

"Not if you were the kind of person who could compartmentalize your life and not let the family part distract you from your goals."

"And I'm not that kind of person?" she asked.

"Are you?"

"No, I guess I'm not."

"The world could forgive a few children from a person who was trying to get women to restrict their childbearing. It might cause awkward moments and persistent questions from skeptics, but the world can overlook inconsistencies. What it can't forgive is failure of leadership."

"I'm not the only person around who can do this. I'm not even the best one and certainly not the most important one. If I got married and retired to domesticity, someone else would step in and carry on the fight."

"Don't deceive yourself. You are important. Without you the battle would be lost."

"That's nonsense," she said, and then her face brightened into a smile. "Oh, I see. Now you're going to give me that prediction."

"I haven't wanted to do it," he said softly, "because knowledge like this—if you believe it—can change people, too. But you are a special person, so special that it frightens me."

"Why me?" she asked. She sounded as if it was frightening her.

"I've asked the same question myself," Johnson said, "and so did Hamlet. 'The time is out of joint. O cursed spite that ever I was born to set it right.' But there are people whose lives have the potential to affect the future more than others. They are possessed by great ideas, taken over by missions larger than themselves: Mostly the founders of religions, but there were also conquerors and kings, political leaders and rebels, occasionally a philosopher, and once in a while an inventor or discoverer who had no intention of changing the world but changed it anyway."

"But I'm not like that," she said.

"Most of them were remarkable people, driven men, some of them bitter, hard, hungry, single-minded.... And you're not like that. But you have the same quality of being possessed by an idea and the ability to pass your possession on to others. Your—forgive me—your remarkable beauty and your renunciation of its traditional values are a part of your total impact on the future, but more important are your concern for other people, your ability to communicate with them at all levels, your excellent mind, your dedication, and most of all your presence. You have the ability, because of who you are and where you stand, to be larger than life, to move people and change the world just by being yourself."

She sighed. "I didn't ask for this. I don't want it."

"Nobody ever asks for it, and you don't have to keep it," Johnson said, "although I have to tell you the future will be an unhappier place if you give it up." He paused and then added, "But knowing the future is not the way to happiness."

She reached across the table and took his hand. "Oh, Bill, it must be worse for you, and I've only been thinking about myself."

"You believe my strange story then?" he asked.

"How can I help but believe," she said. "Your face, your eyes, your wisdom...."

"Then believe this, too. There are other dangers, not simply to you, though that is bad enough, but to what you can accomplish. You trust people—and that is one reason for your success—but you must learn caution, not expose yourself to danger unnecessarily, have people around whose only job is to look after you."

"I thought that was the job you picked out for yourself," she said lightly but as if she was growing to like the idea.

"I've made it my job, but I may not always be around."

"Don't say that!" she said. "I know this is crazy. I found you in an alley this morning, got you as an unwanted employee by noon, and now you've become indispensable. By tomorrow I'll want to marry you." She was joking, but there was an edge of truth to her words that made an expression of something like pain pass across Johnson's face. She patted his hand. "Don't worry, Bill, that wasn't a proposal."

She was exuberant again, and she stood up quickly. The bill had long ago been paid. "I'll race you to People, Limited. If you catch me, maybe there will be a prize."

"Sally, don't. . . ." he began, getting up. "This is a dangerous part of town. Be—"

But she had already threaded her way between tables toward the front door, and he had to follow quickly, trying to catch up. When he reached the front door, he looked quickly down either side of the narrow and poorly lighted street, but she was nowhere to be seen. He went down the flight of worn stone steps and hesitated at the bottom, looking right and left as if he were seeing farther than the nearest streetlight, as if he could peer past the shadowy present into the bright future. He ran quickly to the left, down cobbled pavement, through pools of darkness.

"Sally!" he called. "Sally!"

He heard a muffled sound and raced toward it. "Sally," he said, and stopped at the entrance to a dark alley between old houses. "Tommy? I know you're there, and I know you've got Ms. Franklin."

A boy's voice came from the shadows. "How you know that, man?"

"I have an unusual kind of vision," Johnson said.

"You see that, you see I got a knife at her throat, and I use it, just like that, you make a move." A vague scuffling sound came from a place about ten feet away from Johnson. "And you keep quiet, lady, or you get it now."

"Let her go, Tommy," Johnson said. "Nothing good will come of this—only bad, all bad."

"I can kill her and get you, too. Nobody ever knows— How you know my name?"

"You were in the group that found me this morning in the alley," Johnson said.

"You can't see me now." The voice was hard and suspicious. It seemed less boyish with each passing moment.

"I know a great many things, Tommy," Johnson said earnestly. "I know that you come from a large family, that your father is dead and your mother is sick and your brothers and sisters don't have enough to eat."

"You a cop?" the voice from the shadows asked suspiciously. "You been keeping track of me?"

"I won't lie to you, Tommy. No, I'm all alone. I'm just a man with a peculiar way of knowing what is going to happen. And I have to tell you that the future will be very bad for you if you do to Ms. Franklin what you have in your mind."

"She everything I can't have," the boy said. "I get something. I ought to get something."

"Not this way, Tommy," Johnson said. "That's just violence, not sex. All you'll get is death for yourself and a bad experience for her that may change her life and the lives of a lot of people. And you'll kill your mother. She'll die when she finds out what you've done. And your brothers and sisters—what small chance they have for happiness will be gone."

"Ah-h-h!" the boy's voice snarled, but a note of doubt had crept in. "How you know that stuff?"

"I told you that I have this strange vision," Johnson said evenly. "I have another future for you. You let Ms. Franklin go and tomorrow you go to the place where she works—you know where it is, Tommy, because I saw you watching it this morning—and you ask for a job."

"How they gonna let me have a job after what I done?"

"You haven't done anything yet, Tommy. Ms. Franklin is frightened, but she hasn't been harmed. She understands the kind of life you've had, the anger built up in you, the hate that strikes at anybody. You've seen her before. She's worked in this city with people who are poor and struggling. She wants to make things better."

"Why they hire me?"

"Because I'll ask them to, and Ms. Franklin will ask them."

"I show up, maybe they throw me in jail."

"What for? You haven't done anything yet. And how can you be worse off than you are now?"

"They hire me, what I do?"

"My idea is that you guard Ms. Franklin, keep her from harm. You'd be good at it. You know how it can happen. You know what to look for."

"Not like you, man."

"You have other talents. You could be something. You could make things better, not worse."

"Ah, man, you talk too much," the voice said. It sounded boyish again. And out of the darkness came

Franklin, reeling as if she had been shoved, holding her throat.

Johnson caught her in his arms. "You show up tomorrow," he called after the sound of running feet. "Are you all right?" he asked the woman trembling in his arms.

She held on to him. "Yes," she said. "Yes. Thanks to you."

"He might not have done it."

"I didn't think he would do it. I've seen him around. I didn't think he was dangerous."

"Maybe he wasn't."

"I'm afraid he was."

"Only because he was scared." He led her back down the dark street toward the lights of the busier avenue that crossed it.

"Will he show up tomorrow?"

"There's a good chance."

"You really want me to hire him?"

"It might save him. He might save you."

"Bill," she said and took a deep shuddering breath, "I don't want him to save me. I want it to be you. Always."

They had reached the avenue and turned now toward the brighter lights of the Capitol area and the People, Limited, building. Johnson's hand tightened on her arm. "It can't be that way. Much as I would like it."

Her hand clutched his waist. "What do you mean? Because of what you did? That was a—a crisis?"

"Maybe."

"You might forget?"

"Possibly."

"It was that important?"

"Yes."

"What would have happened?"

"It would have changed you. You would not have lost your commitment, but you would have lost your edge. A little bitterness perhaps, a little hardness, a little suspicion . . . a loss of innocence."

"A loss of you," she said. "That's what I can't endure." She held him tightly to her side as they walked along. "You can stay. You can come with me to India. If you forget, I can make you remember. I think I love you, Bill. I know I can't lose you."

"You mustn't mistake relief and gratitude for love."

"What about your feelings? You aren't just a mechanism for solving the world's problems. You have feelings. You have a right to a little happiness."

"It would make me very happy to stay with you," Johnson said. "And I want you to know that I could have loved you."

" 'Could have'?"

"It seems to me that love doesn't happen in a day. And that's how I live my life. But it's more than that. If I stayed with you, there's a good chance we would fall in love, that you would love me beyond anything else, and that for you I would give up everything."

"What more could people want out of life?"

"Nothing, if they didn't also know that they got their happiness at the world's expense. You see, I would know that to be my wife and bear my children"—"Oh, yes," Sally said—"humanity would have lost its best chance at limiting its size to a number that the world's resources could support. How could I live with such knowledge? How could you?"

"We would forget," she said fiercely.

They had reached the doors of People, Limited. "No, we would never forget. We would be happy—defiantly, guiltily happy—but we would never forget. And I would see all the evils of the world that I might have been able to do something about, and I would feel unrelentingly the need to act—and my love for you would stop me."

"Oh, Bill," she said, and pressed her head tightly against his chest.

"Go to India," he said. "Success awaits you there. You will do great things, and you will find your happiness in doing them, and the future will be a better place for the fact that you have lived. And remember—wherever you go, whatever you do, somewhere in this world there is a man who loves you if he only knew it."

Somewhere above the Pacific Ocean an airliner hurled itself toward India. Far below and far behind a bus crawled through hills toward the plains beyond. On it, by the light of a small reading light in the base of an overhead rack, a man was printing precise words with a pencil on the back of a ticket envelope.

"Your name is Bill Johnson," he wrote. "You have saved the woman who will be the single most important factor in saving the world from overpopulation, and you don't remember. You may read stories in the newspapers about her accomplishments, but you will find no mention of your part in them.

"For this there are several possible explanations. . . ."

After he had finished, he put the envelope in his inside jacket pocket, and turned off the overhead light. Now the bus was completely dark except for the faint glow near the driver. The passenger stared out at the night beyond the windows. Once in a great while a light would appear in the darkness—a farmhouse or some lonely country crossing—and then sweep past to be lost behind, while the empty miles turned under the wheels.

Episode Six
Will-of-the-Wisp

The sun rose behind the mountains like a bloodshot eye peering after the fleeing bus. Dawn should have revealed a fair prospect of fertile farms and grazing animals, but haze lay across the plain and the bus dived into it as if trying to escape a pursuing Polyphemus.

In the seat next to a window, the man who had no name stirred and opened his eyes. They were dark and strangely empty, like the eyes of someone who has been awakened from a dream and does not remember who or where he is. His face was honey-colored and pleasant, good-looking but not memorable. He was not a boy, but his skin was smooth, unlined by time, unmarked by events.

He sat up straighter in his seat and adjusted the gray tweed jacket. A wince crossed his face as if his body had reminded him of a night spent trying to lie flat in a place that inclined only a few degrees from the vertical.

The man looked around the bus at the heads of the other

passengers. Most of them were sleeping or had their eyes closed, but a few stared stonily at the back of the seat ahead of them or with unseeing eyes out the window beside them.

The turning of the wheels on the interstate highway beneath them enclosed the passengers in an environment of unrelenting sound and vibration. The odor of urine and feces soured the air. The man looked toward the rear of the bus where an enclosed cubicle indicated a toilet that had been pushed beyond its capacity.

The man sank back in his seat and looked out the window. The mist swirled as the bus passed. Occasionally it lifted to reveal brief glimpses of the countryside. It looked like a battlefield after all the soldiers had been buried.

Harvest was over. A few stalks of corn stubble remained in the baked fields. But, by the evidence of the scattered stalks, the harvest had been meager. Occasionally, back from the road, could be seen a discouraged farmhouse and deteriorating outbuildings. Rusting machinery or the remains of old cars littered barnyards and the corners of fields. A few animals—bony cattle and horses, forlorn sheep and ever-hopeful goats—tried to forage in dry pastures or licked mud from the bottom of dry ponds.

The man staring out the window looked pained, as if he were gazing not at the landscape passing but beyond that into a circle of the inferno. Even after the fog closed around the bus again, and nothing could be seen, he continued to stare, until finally, as if he had seen too much, he turned away and began to search through his pockets.

Finally, in his inside jacket pocket, he found a ticket

envelope with neat words printed precisely across it in pencil.

"Your name is Bill Johnson," he read. "You have saved the woman who will be the single most important factor in saving the world from overpopulation, and you don't remember. You may read stories in the newspapers about her accomplishments, but you will find no mention of your part in them.

"For this there are several possible explanations, including the likelihood that I may be lying or deceived or insane. But the explanation on which you must act is that I have told you the truth: you are a man who was born in a future that has almost used up all hope; you were sent to this time and place to alter the events that created that future.

"Am I telling the truth? The only evidence you have is your apparently unique ability to foresee consequences—it comes like a vision, not of the future because the future can be changed, but of what will happen if events take their natural course, if someone does not act, if you do not intervene.

"But each time you intervene, no matter how subtly, you change the future from which you came. You exist in this time and outside of time and in the future, and so each change makes you forget.

"I wrote this message last night to tell you what I know, just as I learned about myself this morning by reading a message printed on a piece of cardboard, for I am you and we are one, and we have done this many times before."

The man who now had a name, Bill Johnson, stared down at the envelope as if he was trying to deny its existence and then, with a kind of revulsion, he tore it into small pieces and tossed them into the litter on the floor. He turned to look out the window again. The fog lifted for a moment.

The highway was passing beside a broad river, but the water was mud-colored, as if it had swallowed a thousand farms, and its surface had a gray-green sheen. Nothing moved in or above it. The countryside had given way to shacks that had grown up like toadstools along the flat land alongside the river. Sad-faced children stood among them, clothed in rags, bellies protruding, watching the bus pass their small corner of the world, appearing out of nowhere, disappearing into the unknown.

The shacks evolved into more permanent dwellings; once decent houses, they had long since ceased to care about appearances. Their walls looked as if they had never seen paint, and the bare soil around them was littered with abandoned junk, old boxes, and discarded papers. Factories raised their concrete-and-sheet-metal barricades along the riverbank and, in stinking gushes, exhausted their wastes from big pipes into the sullen flow beneath.

As Johnson watched he saw a remarkable phenomenon: the river began to burn. Flames licked across the surface like red and blue sprites dancing on the water. It was like a sign from whatever fallen angels ruled this particular region. From a distance it seemed marvelous, but as the highway drew the bus closer to the river Johnson could see oily smoke ascending into the clouds hanging close above before the fog closed in again.

Johnson shut his eyes and leaned his head back against the seat as if he was trying to forget what he had seen, but then, as the bus slowed, he opened them again. The bus stopped, and the universe of sound and vibration in which the passengers had existed for so long suddenly ended.

People stirred and irritated voices demanded to know what was going on.

"Are we there?" an older woman asked.

"Breakfast stop, twenty-five minutes," the bus driver announced gruffly.

"That's hardly long enough to wash our hands," a man complained behind Johnson, "much less get rid of enough of this bus stink to be able to eat anything."

"Twenty-five minutes," the bus driver repeated. He opened the door, and the stench of the world outside poured in. It had not been fog but smog, filled with smoke and other irritants, seen and unseen.

"I wasn't hungry anyway," the man said behind Johnson.

But Johnson shifted and stood up. He started down the aisle, and then, as if by afterthought, reached back and took a suitcase out of the rack above his head.

"Just a stop, mister," the bus driver growled as he saw the suitcase.

Johnson looked at the diner on the frontage road beside the burning river. It was not in much better repair than the shacks and decayed houses they had passed. "EAT," read a sign above the front door. "Fine Food," said an unlighted neon sign in a fly-specked window. Whatever fine foods had ever existed inside the building had long ago turned into wastes.

A double row of gas pumps lined a cracked concrete island where the bus stood, and a small building housed a sleepy attendant and a couple of doors that said "Men" and "Women." "Thought I might clean up," Johnson said. "Maybe even change."

"Thirty-five people gotta use them johns," the driver snarled.

"I won't be long," Johnson said, and brushed past,

walking toward the door marked "Men." But he kept walking and found himself along the riverbank where a trail had been beaten through weeds and brush. On his left was the burning river. On his right was an impenetrable forest of scrub trees.

The purposefulness with which Johnson had left the bus deserted him there, as if he had only enough willpower for a single act. His shoulders drooped, and he stared without expression at the dirt path as he put one foot in front of the other.

He came upon the dump along the riverside about midday. The city had grown around him. The skyscrapers were still in the distance, but the buildings on the other side of the river and those he could glimpse above the riverbank on his side were larger and more permanent. The dump was an area where the bank had widened or been dug out. Trucks pulled up to the road above and let loose small avalanches of trash. Dust billowed. Pickups and cars contributed their sly plastic sacks. The place had a stink of rot and moist decay that was different from the general odor of industrial effluents and machine exhausts. The dump odor was so omnipresent that it became the way the world was and was soon forgotten.

Johnson put down his suitcase and rubbed his elbow. He was about to sit on the suitcase when a voice spoke behind him.

"Welcome to hell!" a man said easily.

Johnson turned. Behind him stood a small man in the remains of what might once have been a gray business suit. But he had no tie on the ragged collar of his white shirt, the suit was torn and droopy, and he carried a shopping sack. He was white-haired and had several days'

CRISIS! 195

growth of white beard on his face, but his eyes were blue and bright and he gave the illusion of being dapper.

"Thanks," Johnson said. He smiled briefly.

"Are you abandoning hope," the other said, "or just slumming?"

"I don't know," Johnson said.

"A bit of indecision never hurt anybody in this place," the other man said. "Most people don't arrive with suitcases, however," he went on. "A few got knapsacks or bedrolls. What you got in there? Going to share? Or hide it out?"

"I don't know," Johnson said. "I mean, I don't know what I've got in here." He knelt down beside the suitcase and opened it. "I'd be glad to share."

The little man gave him an odd glance. "You're a strange duck," he said. "Stranger than most." Then he gave his attention to what Johnson was revealing in the suitcase: a few shirts, underclothes, pairs of socks—all serviceable but worn. "Thanks," he said, "but I'll keep my own. Fit better, too. Some might steal those, however, even here, where people are honester than usual. Better keep them close-by."

Johnson closed the suitcase and laid it flat. Then he emptied his pockets on it: a few coins, a pocket comb, a bus ticket to Kansas City, and a billfold that contained five bills—two ones, two fives, and a ten. He also had a plastic-encased social security card made out to Bill Johnson and a Visa charge card made out to the same name.

"Help yourself," Johnson said, gesturing at the little pile of belongings as if he had no sense of ownership.

The little man leaned over and gently extracted one dollar bill from the heap. "More would lead me in the wrong direction," he said cheerfully. "I'd begin to want things again. You'd better put the rest away where they won't easily be found. Particularly that." He indicated the charge card with his toe. "A person could do a lot of damage to himself with one of those."

When Johnson had stowed things away, the little man said, "Now that we've got rid of the preliminaries, maybe we should introduce ourselves. I'm Sylvester Harding Vines, Jr. But people around here call me 'Duke.' "

"Bill Johnson," Johnson said.

They shook hands formally.

"What did you do before . . . ?" Johnson looked around the dump.

Duke raised a small, white hand. "You can get away with a lot of things around a place like this, but one question nobody asks is what you did before or why you're here. All of us got reasons, some guilty, some painful, and people who go poking around are considered antisocial."

Johnson didn't say anything.

"Having said that," Duke went on brightly, "I must add that you seem a bit confused. Something you need help with?"

Johnson took a deep breath as if he was about to speak and then shook his head. "I don't know."

"If it comes. . . ." Duke said comfortably. "Meanwhile, maybe you'd like a bite to eat." He fished around in the shopping sack and came out with a couple of apples. "Got a bruised spot or two," he said, "but you can eat around those if you're particular."

Johnson picked up his suitcase and they walked along in the direction Johnson had been going, toward the city, munching on their apples. Johnson pointed at the flames on the river. "How long has that been going on?"

"Off and on for the past ten years. It burns out in a few

hours—and then the pollution starts building up again. Nobody seems to care. Seems to be happening more often now."

"Nobody does anything about it?"

The little man shrugged. "Gets rid of the pollution better than most things. Oh, used to be the fireboats would get out here and try to smother it with chemicals and such, but that seemed to be worse than letting it burn. Bother you?"

"I look at it and see a world dying in its own wastes," Johnson said, as if he were a million miles away.

"No worse than a lot of things," Duke said. "But I can see that it might depress somebody who had a future. You got a future?"

"I don't know," Johnson said.

"A whole lot of things you don't know," Duke said, giving him a sidelong glance. "But that's your business. Come on. I'll introduce you to some of the guys."

They sat with their backs against a clay bluff that had been blackened and hardened by old fires whose odors still lingered, but they were difficult to distinguish from the fire over which the communal evening meal had been cooked. The fire still burned fifteen feet away toward the river, and a large, sooty pot still hung from an improvised metal support above the fire. The pot had been salvaged some months ago, Johnson had been told, by Smitty, a tall, wiry man of indeterminate age who was the luckiest junk picker of the whole group. In the pot was some mulligan stew left over after everybody had eaten their fill out of old tin cans and assorted metal objects beaten into the shape of plates and cups.

Almost everyone had contributed something to the meal

except Johnson: a few potatoes here, a couple of carrots and turnips there, an onion, a clove of garlic, a piece of meat into whose origin and age nobody inquired, a battered can of tomatoes opened with a hunting knife, a few shakes of salt and pepper from a hoarded store, and other assorted seasonings.

"That was good!" Johnson had said, as he wiped up the last of his meal with a piece of stale French bread.

"Meals eaten in the open air and all that," Duke had said.

Johnson had met some of the other dropouts. Most of them were men, and all except one or two were middle-aged or older. The young ones had something wrong behind their eyes. The older ones had simply given up on any kind of future. They wanted to think no farther ahead than a few minutes. But those minutes they filled with useful activities.

Many of them searched for usable items in the trash dumped by the big trucks. These they cleaned as best they could and sold to secondhand stores for pennies; some they repaired with surprising skill and used themselves. One craggy old man spent his days turning objects he found in the trash into strange sculpture, which he left along the riverbank until mischievous boys or high water destroyed them. He did not seem to care. He contributed little or nothing to the evening meal, but he was fed anyway.

Some scavenged through the dumpsters of nearby supermarkets and restaurants for edible materials too damaged or old or stale to sell. They would return, like Santa Clauses, with their sacks of plenty. The women seemed particularly good at this. The women were all old. They had the swollen joints and painful movements of arthritis, but they seemed otherwise in good health.

None of them spent money for anything but medicine or tobacco. When food ran short, they went, reluctantly, to soup kitchens and other charities.

The rest of them had now scattered to different parts of the area adjacent to the dump. Actually, Duke had explained, it was over the dump. This part had been filled up and covered with dirt. Beneath was a midden waiting for some future archeologist to unearth its treasures.

The river had stopped burning, but Johnson still stared at it as if it held an answer he was seeking.

"Is this what you were looking for?" Duke said.

Johnson stirred. "No. But maybe it's better."

"There's worse. That's for sure." The distant firelight cast a ruddy glow against Duke's face. He looked as if he was thinking about a place that was worse.

"What do you do in the winter?"

"Some go south like migrating birds. Some find an old building to hole up in. There's a lot of those around. Nobody fixes things anymore, and it costs money to tear them down. Some just tough it out here, with boxes and shanties. A few die, some from exposure. But there's always replacements, and everybody dies sooner or later."

"Nobody tries to help?"

"Once in a while a social worker will poke around, once in a while a do-gooder will remember the forgotten people and try to rescue us, once in a while a church will try to redeem us. More often the cops will bust our heads and try to send us somewhere else. We always come back, because this is home. Is this home for you?"

"I wish it were," Johnson said.

"There's always room. If you aren't particular, you can make out on what society throws away."

"I can see that," Johnson said, "and it's very attractive. But I think there's something wrong with me."

"There's something wrong with all of us here, at least the way the rest of the world looks at it. We've given up, and it feels good."

"No, there's something wrong with me the way people here look at it," Johnson said. Then, as if changing the subject, he asked, "Can you look out there and see how things are going to be?"

"Not if I don't want to," Duke said. "And I don't want to. That's why I'm here. I got tired of worrying about the way things were going to turn out: kids, marriage, career, the stock market, the economy, the country, the world. . . . Once you start worrying there's no place to stop unless you just stop entirely."

"I can see that," Johnson said. "Maybe it's just me."

"You really see things?"

Johnson put his right hand in front of his eyes. "I look out there and see a world that can no longer even breathe: people choking, gasping for air, and each breath sears their lungs. The food is poisoned and the water is ruined; the world is burning up with heat it can't get rid of."

"You really see this. You don't just imagine it."

"I really see it," Johnson said, "and I have a desperate need to do something about it."

"You do have a problem, friend," Duke said. "I'll tell you what: in my previous life I used to be a physician. I couldn't cure myself. But I have a few acquaintances who still are in the business, including a psychiatrist who owes me a favor or two. In the morning, if you can lend me a quarter, I will make a telephone call and see if I can get you some help."

They sat for a while as if thinking about it while the

night grew darker and the river sloshed greasily against the bank. Suddenly, in the distance, brief blue fire appeared above the dump and skipped away like a fairy converting trash into treasure.

"What's that?" Johnson asked. "Has the river started burning again?"

"No, that's the dump. It's a will-of-the-wisp, what some people call St. Elmo's fire. Used to be seen around marshes with its decaying vegetation. Now we see it quite often here as garbage, newspapers, and other vegetable matter is converted into today's version of marsh gas."

"What's marsh gas?"

"Methane. Also called firedamp when formed in mines. CH_4. The principal ingredient in natural gas. Some places are digging gas wells in old dumps to recover the usable methane."

" 'Will-of-the-wisp,' " Johnson mused.

"Also means an elusive or deceptive object. The story goes that people used to pursue it across a marsh until they drowned."

"Yes," Johnson said, as if he were agreeing how easy it would be. "Do you think your friend can help me?"

"Well, now, I don't have much faith in 'help' anymore. The question is, Do *you* have faith?"

Duke's friend was a woman. She was a strikingly attractive woman in her middle to late thirties, perhaps, with black hair streaked with premature gray strands, black arching eyebrows, dark brown eyes that seemed to hide in caves and then leap out upon the unwary passerby, and vivid coloring in cheeks and lips. She would not have looked out of place in a gypsy caravan with a bandana tied around her head. She occupied her office completely, filling it with herself from wall to wall so that patients did not so much enter the room as come into her web.

Her name was Roggero, and she spoke in a mixture of deep, resonant phrases and pregnant pauses that her patients hastened to fill with revelations. "Dr. Vines is a remarkable man," she said in her gypsy voice. "A remarkable man. He is not an old man. Did you know that? No older than his late fifties. He likes to let people think he is older, because the world does not expect as much of them. Society lets older men alone. But he is still a better man than anyone I know.

"He was a man of great personal power. He was not just a physician. He could cure people, yes. But he shaped people's lives. He shaped government and industry. He shaped this city. He was the force behind the building of this complex. He worked to make life better. He helped people. He is responsible for my being here. The ghetto family that took care of me after my parents were killed in an accident brought me to him for treatment and he saw the anger in me, and he got me schooling and training and he channeled that anger into helping others. He has had much tragedy in his life, and if he is where he is today, that is his decision and his story to tell. What you should know if I am to help you is that I would do anything for him. Anything.

"We were lovers. Would you think that? This little, white-haired man and this strong, young woman of wild passions. Ah, but you do not know him. No one really knows him, even me, and no one knows what a man is like with a woman. But I know him best. So, I will help you. Dr. Vines has asked me to help you—for what reason I do not know, and I do not care. There will be no talk of money.

"You will fall in love with me if these sessions go on very long. That is perfectly natural. It may be that we will become lovers, and that should not bother you. All of these things must be understood before we start. You should know me, just as I must learn to know you. Now, tell me what troubles you."

So Johnson, who had received all her remarkable confidences with the face of a listener, told her what troubled him. They sat in her office in a tall building in the center of the city, she in a padded chair behind a darkly gleaming desk that had nothing on it except a pad of ruled yellow paper and a gold-colored fountain pen, and he in an upholstered armchair beside the desk. He talked in a low but clear voice about his experience of waking up the morning before in a bus and not knowing who he was or where he was going, of staring out the window at the desolate countryside, of finding a message.

"Do you have that message with you?" she asked.

"I tore it up and threw it away."

"Why did you do that?"

"It suddenly seemed too much."

"In what way?"

"I could not believe what it seemed to tell me."

"And what was that?"

"That I came from the future. That I intervened in the problems of the present to solve them, to make the future better. That whenever I changed things I forgot who I was, and that was why I kept leaving messages. That this had happened many times before."

"If you looked around at the world, you would not see much evidence that someone exists such as you describe."

"Yes, it's crazy."

"On the other hand," she said, "the world is in a bad condition. Someone like that would be a godsend."

"There's no reason to think he could exist."

"No," she said. "That is the difficult part. But it is easy to understand why a person looking out at the world might feel compelled to do something about it."

"Yes."

"Might even feel in some way selected."

"You're saying that my delusion is natural."

"No delusions are natural. They are a failure to recognize and cope with reality. Sometimes, when conditions are bad and no solution seems possible, delusions may be an understandable response. People with systems of delusions are often happy and can even function normally so long as those delusions do not come into conflict with reality. You are troubled because your belief system has come into conflict with what you believe to be reality."

"What I believe to be reality?"

"There are all kinds of realities, and none of us can be sure we share the same one, if there is one. But we have not established yet that you have a delusion."

"What else could it be?"

"That is what we must determine before we can treat it. But you must have some evidence to support what that note told you, or you would simply have dismissed it."

"I have—visions," Johnson said with a helpless spreading of his palms. "That is what the note said, and it seemed like confirmation."

"What kind of visions?"

"Like a glimpse of another view of what I've been looking at. But it's grimmer. Darker. As if it's the future, or the way the future will be unless someone does something about it. It's disorienting. Makes you dizzy at first, like a briefly glimpsed scene that's the same but different, thrown into the midst of a movie you're watching, and then you get used to it—or at least I did. You learn to ignore it for practical purposes. But it's what the vision implies that is disturbing."

"What does it imply?"

"At first I thought everybody saw visions like that, but I've asked, and nobody admits it."

"You think they're lying?"

Johnson slowly shook his head. "I hoped they were. Do you ever see such things?"

"I'm sorry. Are you seeing them now?" Johnson nodded. "What do you see?"

Johnson looked away from her and stood up. He walked to the window and gazed down toward the street far below. Yesterday's fog had lifted, but the air was hazy and tinged with yellow. Vehicles moved like brightly colored beetles along the street, adding their exhausts to the general level of pollution.

"The smog thickens," Johnson said in a monotone. "The automobiles dwindle, like dinosaurs dying out. Garbage and trash pile up in the streets. Nobody takes it away. Children and old people die in the streets. They fall over. They gasp. They stop breathing. People are robbed and raped and murdered. Plagues break out. People flee, but the countryside is only a little better. Finally everything is still."

Dr. Roggero was silent for several minutes. "And you want to stop seeing these things? You want to be relieved of the compulsion to do something about them?"

Johnson turned back to her. "Oh, very much," he said.

* * *

Dr. Roggero's office building was one of a group of buildings clustered around a plaza. The group included a theater, a conference center, a hotel, and a collection of shops, all of them served by an underground garage. In the center a fountain sent plumes of spray high in the air, and occasionally, when the wind was strong, sprinkled the nearest benches or passersby.

The plaza was clean. Uniformed attendants moved between the benches and the stone trash containers with broom and hose, with polishing cloth and plastic bag. The plaza was like an oasis in the midst of a desert, but even here the air itself was visible as fumes rolled through it from the street and smoke and fog blew in from the river.

Johnson stopped just outside the entrance to the office building as if adjusting from the air-conditioned fantasy he had left to the reality ahead. He was neat. Dr. Vines, Duke, had shown him how to use the public restrooms to make himself presentable and admired the fact that he didn't need to shave. "Vinya won't care," he said, "but the people in uniform, the elevator attendants and the receptionists, may give you trouble. Always watch out for people in uniform. It gives them delusions of power."

As Johnson was crossing the plaza heading back toward the river, a woman's voice came ringing across the concrete and stone. "Bill!" it called. "Bill Johnson!"

Johnson turned. Behind him, hurrying across the plaza from the conference building, was a woman. She was cool and blonde and beautiful in a gray, summer-weight dress. She carried a folder under one arm and had a gray leather bag slung over the other. Her eyes were gray and appraising as she got closer.

"Bill," she said breathlessly. "I thought it was you, but I couldn't be certain."

CRISIS!

He looked at her courteously but without recognition. "Do we know each other?" he asked.

And at the same moment she said, "You don't recognize me, do you?"

She laughed with just a trace of embarrassment and broke off and looked at him. "You haven't changed," she said. "Maybe a little sadder."

"I'm sorry," he said. "I should know who you are, but I seem to have forgotten a great deal. It's a mental problem. I'm seeking treatment."

She put a hand on the sleeve of his jacket. "Oh, Bill," she said. "You told me that you would forget me, and I didn't believe you. I couldn't believe you. We were very close once. I left you a tape recorder with a message on it, don't you remember? Of course you don't remember.

"Look, I'm rattling on, I know. I'm not like that usually. I don't act flustered and helpless, but I never thought I'd see you again. I was hurt and angry and then sad, after what we'd been through—and now you don't know me. It's all too much."

"I know," he said.

"It must be worse for you," she said. People were beginning to stop near them and stare curiously at this unusual couple. "Oh, no, not worse. Just different." She caught her lower lip between her teeth as if to stop the words from coming out. "You don't know how many times I have thought I saw you and called or run after a man, only to discover he was a stranger. And now, of course, to you I am a stranger. If we could just have a few moments together—but it wouldn't be any good now. I'm too upset, and I—"

She paused as if trying to pull herself together and talk calmly. "You are Bill Johnson, aren't you?"

"Yes."

"I accept the fact that you don't know me. My name is Frances Miller. I'm the managing editor of the Associated Press, and I'm here for a conference. On what else? Pollution. I'm staying in the Hilton there. Remember the Hilton? In New York? . . . No, of course you don't. I've got to rest. But I want you to promise me something: come see me tonight when I'm myself. In memory of what we did together, even though you don't remember it."

"I'll try," he said.

"Oh, god!" she said, turning away. "I know you'll try. But will it be enough?" And she almost ran toward the entrance of the hotel.

They sat once more with their backs to the bluff, Johnson and Duke, watching the river burn in the dusk. Sometimes the colored sprites ran across the water and onto the land, and sometimes the will-of-the-wisps seemed to dance to the water's edge and hesitate, as if their magic ended where the river began, and then skip out to join the water spirits.

"A marvelous woman, Vinya," Duke said. "A little fiery at times. A bit overpowering perhaps. But I don't mind that in a woman. Some might."

"I liked her," Johnson said.

"But is she going to help you?"

"She says she is."

"She's confident, too. Maybe too confident. But then she hasn't had to face up to failure. You have to be confident, though, if you're going to succeed in the help business."

"I can see that," Johnson said. "If I really believed in my delusions, if I really thought I was in the help business, I'd have to appear confident, even when I wasn't. Faith is what it's all about."

"That's true."

"And the pollution business, that's one big problem."

"If you can see how it ends up, the way you do," Duke agreed. "But then the things you can't do anything about, you don't want to think about. That includes most things."

"What if you could do something about it, though?"

"That would be a difficult situation, wouldn't it?" Duke said. "But pollution isn't like that. It's a natural consequence of industrialization. It starts off small, when it doesn't matter, when the 'sinks'—the oceans and the air—seem bottomless, and then it builds until the sinks are filled up."

"Can't people stop the way they start?" Johnson asked. "People don't want to die. They don't want to run out of air or water or food. They don't want to kill birds and fish and animals."

"Not unless they can enjoy it or profit from it. Trouble is, the profit comes from doing it, and it costs too much to stop. Any one person who stops doesn't solve the problem; he just goes broke himself. It's what a man named Garrett Hardin calls 'the tragedy of the commons.'

"When people share something like a pasture, where everybody can graze their animals as much as they wish, if too many cattle are added to the pasture it will be overgrazed and destroyed, and nobody will be able to use it. Adding one more animal, or two or three, doesn't injure the pasture. But it increases individual profits, so the rational act of each herdsman is to increase his herd, because the effect of his actions are minimal on the pasture but improve his personal situation significantly. It's like that with the world."

"What about government? Shouldn't it think about the welfare of the group?"

"It should, and there was a period in the Sixties and Seventies when government was doing something about it, and conditions were improving. But government isn't just people. It is industries and corporations and smaller units of government, and the constituencies for the general welfare are never as vocal or as well-financed as the special interests. And people have never been good at putting off a present benefit for a future good. The general welfare is abstract and unfocused; making a profit or avoiding a loss is specific and sharp.

"No," Duke said, and laughed. "I'm reminded of a reply that Ralph G. Ingersoll, the famous agnostic, made to the fundamentalist minister who baited him with the question as to how he would improve the world if he were God. 'Why,' Ingersoll said, 'I'd make good health catching instead of sickness.' I reckon we won't get rid of pollution until we can make a profit out of it."

They looked out past the firelight toward one of the old man's sculptures. It had been put together from driftwood and automobile parts, and it looked like a crucified robot.

Once more they sat in Dr. Roggero's office. She was like a goddess presiding over the altar of her desk, he like a worshipper in the chair beside it.

She toyed with a slender metal letter opener as she studied his face and said, "Dr. Lindner reported a case that later become famous in which he cured a patient by falling in with his delusions and then convincing him of the fallacies of his logic."

"But I already know the fallacies of my delusion," Johnson said.

"Exactly. And you merely want to be rid of them. What if I told you to forget about them, and merely go on with your life, accepting the fact that you have this mild delusion that seems to do no harm?"

"I could do that," Johnson said. "But what about my visions? And what about my feelings of guilt?"

"Why should you feel guilty? You know that you did not come from the future."

"Certainly the likelihood is very small," Johnson said.

"But it is still a possibility?"

"Isn't it?"

"Of course. But then so are the bases of every other delusion. The problem is, if we act upon them, we run into inconsistencies."

"My delusion has no inconsistencies. It is only unlikely. What can one man do in the face of so many problems? How can one person make a difference when pollution is so omnipresent?"

"If everybody felt like that, nothing would ever get done."

"The fallacy of the irrelevant individual makes a nice complement to the tragedy of the commons," Johnson said. "But I have heard of such things as catalysts, substances that make chemical reactions possible without participating in them. If they are present, the reaction proceeds. Without them, nothing happens. Maybe there are comparable situations among people. Maybe it takes only one person to get something going, to make a difference. It's ridiculous to think that I am that sort of person, but knowing how bad situations are going to become, or the possibility that I know, means that I must feel guilt if I don't act."

"Do you know what your situation reminds me of?

'For God so loved the world, that he gave his only begotten Son. . . .' "

"You think I have a Christ complex?"

"You suffer for the sins of mankind," she said drily.

"Not on purpose," Johnson said. "I don't think of myself as Christ. I'm just a poor suffering bastard caught in a psychological trap not of my making. And I'd like to get free."

" 'Lord, if it be thy will, let these things pass from me,' " she said.

"I don't feel in any way special," Johnson said, "—except that I have this vision. I don't feel divine. I don't feel like the Son of God or the son of man. But how can one see the condition of the world and not feel guilty?"

"A certain amount of guilt is healthy," Dr. Roggero said. "It keeps us from committing crimes. It's society's way of teaching us how to be good citizens and our parents' way of teaching us how to be good people. A person without guilt is a monster. It's only when we feel unnecessary or excessive guilt that it becomes neurosis. To feel guilty about conditions you did not create and cannot change is unnecessary and excessive."

"Thanks," Johnson said, "but it isn't enough."

"I do not like to recommend radical measures," Dr. Roggero said, "but this is a special case. You are impatient, and I do not have the kind of time to devote to this case as might be necessary if we were to proceed with discussion and analysis. Successes have been reported, however, by such brute means as electrical shock or chemical counterparts."

"Would they work?" Johnson said quietly.

"There is a good chance," she said, studying his face.

He took a deep breath. "I want to go ahead with it."

CRISIS! 213

"You will have to sign papers, authorizations, maybe commitments."

"I'll sign them."

"You realize that you may not be the same person afterward."

"In what way?"

"It isn't customary to put it this way, but the kind of person you are will not exist afterward."

"What kind of person am I?"

She looked at him as if she was seeing him not as a patient but as a person. "You are a kind and thoughtful person, a reasonable man, a good listener, a responsible person. You are a good man who may be overly concerned about doing good, but that is a benign condition. The world would be a better place if there were more people like you. There is a legend that Charlie Chaplin went to a psychiatrist for treatment, and that the psychiatrist refused because curing the neuroses might destroy the underlying motivations of his art. Do you know I might feel guilty if I helped you do this?"

"If I were the kind of person you describe," Johnson said slowly, "I might be able to cope with it. If I could really do something about pollution. . . ."

"How do you know you can't?"

"It just seems so—" He sighed. "—Overpowering."

"There is one other possibility." She seemed to hesitate, as if she did not want to give him false hope. "There must be people who knew you before you lost your memory. There must be records: social security records, credit records, birth records, school records. We go through the world leaving trails on paper, like so many snails. . . . If you could discover something that would confirm or deny the information on the piece of paper in your pocket. . . ."

"Yes," he said, looking up. "I could do that. That would help, wouldn't it, if I knew." He stood up suddenly as if he had just thought of something. "Doctor, I've got to leave, to find somebody. Could you get in touch with Duke, with Dr. Vines. Ask him to come here to your office— Are you free over the lunch hour?"

"Yes. But I don't know—"

"That's two hours from now. If you can't find him, then I will search him out. But I would like him here. And thank you—thank you for your patience!"

She looked up at him, clearly surprised at how the office over which she presided so completely had been removed from her control, and then she nodded, accepting his independence.

When Johnson returned he had a woman with him. She was cool, blonde, tailored, and puzzled. Dr. Roggero was seated at her desk, but her attention was directed toward the couch against the wall. On it Duke was sitting, but he had shaved, cleaned his suit, and combed his hair. He looked almost like the physician he once had been. He grimaced apologetically at Johnson. "I could not let Vinya see what a bum I had become. But you have a lady with you. . . ."

"This is Frances Miller. She says she knew me once."

"What's going on?" Miller demanded. She turned to Johnson. "You didn't come to see me last night."

"I thought only pain would come of it. I was so wrapped up in my own problems that I couldn't see yours."

"And now you grab me as I come out of a meeting and pull me upstairs like this. . . ." she continued.

"He needs you," Dr. Roggero said.

At that, Miller's face changed from anger to concern.

"He is a troubled man," the psychiatrist said.

"What's the matter?" Miller said, turning to Johnson.

"I need to know," he said with intensity. "What did we do?"

She looked at the vivid woman behind the desk and the white-haired little man sitting on the sofa. The man smiled and nodded. The woman stared at her. "You want them to know?"

"You said, when we met in the plaza below, 'in memory of what we did together.' That wasn't the way you would have described a personal experience."

"No," she said, looking down and then up at his face. "But it may create problems for you."

"They must be better than the ones I have," he said. "I think I'm crazy."

"Oh, no," Miller said. "You're not. You're—" She stopped again.

"What did we do?"

"We stopped World War III," she said. "You and me and a young fellow named Tom Logan."

Dr. Roggero's office had been audience to many revelations, but the implications of Miller's statement produced a silence that may have outdistanced any of them.

Duke broke it. "Johnson, my boy, you're not crazy. But you may have a more serious problem."

Johnson grinned lopsidedly as if he recognized the truth of Duke's remark. "Which would I rather be? A crazy Don Quixote? Or a sane one?"

"Are you going to tell me what's going on?" Miller demanded.

"In a few minutes," Johnson said, "I will go with you to a quiet spot where we can talk, and I will tell you everything I know. It isn't much, because all I remember about myself starts two days ago. It can't be the same between us as it once must have been. If we were intimate"—she looked down at the floor and then up into his eyes—"I cannot hope for that again. I cannot even imagine it. But I can answer your questions, as you have answered mine and perhaps will answer more."

"We can make it the way it was before," she said fiercely.

"I like you," he said admiringly. "You are a person of conviction and accomplishment. But I must do something now that will destroy what few bridges we have been able to rebuild."

"No," she said.

But he turned to Duke and said, "When Dr. Roggero mentioned solving the pollution problem, I suddenly had a vision of a world free from wastes. Things I saw, things you said, began to fall into place."

"What kind of things?" Duke said. "I certainly didn't intend to be a problem solver. I'm not one of the help people."

"Oh, but you are," Johnson said. "You pretend not to be, but you can't keep from being the kind of person you are."

"That's what I keep telling you, Sylvie," Dr. Roggero said. "All the pretending in the world can't conceal that even from someone who has known you only a few days."

"You helped me. You helped Dr. Roggero. You have helped thousands of people. You help the dropouts at the dump. And now it's time to put yourself back in the help business officially."

Duke's face turned hard. "Never! You don't know what you're asking. There are things in my life. . . ."

"Would you trade it for mine?" Johnson asked. "Would you like to forget everything every few days?"

Duke was silent.

"The will-of-the-wisp," Johnson said. "A symbol of pollution. But some places, you said, were using marsh gas to do useful work. The dropouts at the dump. They exist by turning refuse into usable materials. They live on the wastes of society. Let's turn them into a resource."

"What do you mean?" Duke asked. He was skeptical, but he was listening.

"Let's turn wastes into a resource," Johnson said. "Wastes are only materials that nobody has found a use for. Let's set up viable commercial operations to find uses for wastes. You said that pollution would not be cleaned up until it became profitable. Let's find a way to make it profitable."

"That's a big job," Duke said.

"It's a job for scavengers. You can give people like that a purpose. Maybe a scavenger is only a person who hasn't found what he or she is good for. Give them a purpose. Give them status. Give them a job: cleaning up the environment."

"Not everything can be cleaned up that way," Duke said.

"I know it can't," Johnson said. "You believe the motivation to make a profit is more trustworthy than the motivation to do good. All right. Find a way to make a profit. It doesn't have to be a big profit. But there's another part to the profit motive: the desire to minimize loss. That's where Frances Miller comes in."

"Me?" she said.

"I'm sure your meetings here have discussed Federal legislation, and most of that has focused on forbidding pollution in various ways and various degrees. Mostly polluters have tried to find loopholes or lax enforcement."

"That's true," Miller admitted, "but I don't see what—"

"Let the polluters pollute," Johnson said, "but charge them for the privilege."

"How can any fee compensate for polluting everybody else's environment?" Dr. Roggero asked.

"Wait!" Miller said. "Let him talk."

"You adjust the fee so that in the end it is cheaper not to pollute. It works better than absolute abolition because it is cheaper to enforce and leaves the decision about antipollution measures to the polluter, who is in the best position to know what to do and how to do it."

"But what about Duke's group?" Dr. Roggero asked.

"And all the others like it," Johnson said. "Because this is a way to redeem not only material but human wastes. The fees that are collected from the polluters will go to subsidize the products of Duke's operations until they are self-supporting."

"Do you think it could work?" Duke said.

"If somebody makes it work," Johnson said.

"It might work," Miller said. "I'd be willing to help, and other news media could be persuaded to work on public awareness and political action."

"You could do it," Dr. Roggero said to Duke.

" 'We make money on what you throw away,' " Duke mused. "Might make people think about what they're throwing away. 'Your by-products are our raw materials.' It could be interesting."

"You'll do it, then?" Johnson asked.

Duke did not answer directly but said, "What about you? It's your idea. You could do it."

"If things work out according to the message I read

a couple of mornings ago," Johnson said, "I will start a new life tomorrow. A new challenge. A new crisis. A new vision of what might be, or what ought to be."

"No," Miller said faintly. Her hand went out to him.

"It must be difficult for those whose lives touch mine," Johnson said, "but my existence only looks painful from the outside. I can never see it from there. Each few days I earn the balm of forgetfulness. Only when I doubt. . . ."

"I can fix that," Miller said.

Johnson sat on his suitcase beside the shabby diner at which he had disembarked three days ago. He looked out over the river. It was not burning now. It would burn again, no doubt, but less and less often, perhaps, as Dr. Vines's operation and the anti-pollution fee system began to take effect. Discarded wastes still were everywhere. The odor of decay still filled the air. But the fog had lifted. No doubt it was a coincidence, but already it seemed as if the air was clearer and more breathable.

Johnson looked down at the ring on his finger that a jeweler had prepared to Frances Miller's specifications. It was made of gold. On the flattened surface was the word "Crisis!" On the inside of the ring was engraved, "It's up to you."

Johnson waited without impatience to resume the journey he had interrupted to a destination he no longer remembered.

GORDON R. DICKSON

- [ ] 53068-3 Hoka! (with Poul Anderson) $2.95
  53069-1 Canada $3.50

- [ ] 53556-1 Sleepwalkers' World $2.95
  53557-X Canada $3.50

- [ ] 53564-2 The Outposter $2.95
  53565-0 Canada $3.50

- [ ] 48525-5 Planet Run $2.75
  with Keith Laumer

- [ ] 48556-5 The Pritcher Mass $2.75

- [ ] 48576-X The Man From Earth $2.95

- [ ] 53562-6 The Last Master $2.95
  53563-4 Canada $3.50

- [ ] 53550-2 BEYOND THE DAR AL-HARB $2.95
  53551-0 Canada $3.50

- [ ] 53558-8 SPACE WINNERS $2.95
  53559-6 Canada $3.50

- [ ] 53552-9 STEEL BROTHER $2.95
  53553-7 Canada $3.50

Buy them at your local bookstore or use this handy coupon:
Clip and mail this page with your order

TOR BOOKS—Reader Service Dept.
49 W. 24 Street, 9th Floor, New York, NY 10010

Please send me the book(s) I have checked above. I am enclosing
$_____ (please add $1.00 to cover postage and handling).
Send check or money order only—no cash or C.O.D.'s.

Mr./Mrs./Miss _____
Address _____
City _____ State/Zip _____
Please allow six weeks for delivery. Prices subject to change without notice.

POUL ANDERSON
Winner of 7 Hugos and 3 Nebulas

☐	53088-8	CONFLICT	$2.95
	53089-6		Canada $3.50
☐	48527-1	COLD VICTORY	$2.75
☐	48517-4	EXPLORATIONS.	$2.50
☐	48515-8	FANTASY	$2.50
☐	48550-6	THE GODS LAUGHED	$2.95
☐	48579-4	GUARDIANS OF TIME	$2.95
☐	53567-7	HOKA! (with Gordon R. Dickson)	$2.75
	53568-5		Canada $3.25
☐	48582-4	LONG NIGHT	$2.95
☐	53079-9	A MIDSUMMER TEMPEST	$2.95
	53080-2		Canada $3.50
☐	48553-0	NEW AMERICA	$2.95
☐	48596-4	PSYCHOTECHNIC LEAGUE	$2.95
☐	48533-6	STARSHIP	$2.75
☐	53073-X	TALES OF THE FLYING MOUNTAINS	$2.95
	53074-8		Canada $3.50
☐	53076-4	TIME PATROLMAN	$2.95
	53077-2		Canada $3.50
☐	48561-1	TWILIGHT WORLD	$2.75
☐	53085-3	THE UNICORN TRADE	$2.95
	53086-1		Canada $3.50
☐	53081-0	PAST TIMES	$2.95
	53082-9		Canada $3.50

Buy them at your local bookstore or use this handy coupon:
Clip and mail this page with your order

TOR BOOKS—Reader Service Dept.
49 W. 24 Street, 9th Floor, New York, NY 10010

Please send me the book(s) I have checked above. I am enclosing
$_____ (please add $1.00 to cover postage and handling).
Send check or money order only—no cash or C.O.D.'s.

Mr./Mrs./Miss _____
Address _____
City _____ State/Zip _____
Please allow six weeks for delivery. Prices subject to change without notice.

HARRY HARRISON

☐	48505-0	A Transatlantic Tunnel, Hurrah!	$2.50
☐	48540-9	The Jupiter Plague	$2.95
☐	48565-4	Planet of the Damned	$2.95
☐	48557-3	Planet of No Return	$2.75
☐	48031-8	The QE2 Is Missing	$2.95
☐	48554-9	A Rebel in Time	$3.50

Buy them at your local bookstore or use this handy coupon:
Clip and mail this page with your order

TOR BOOKS—Reader Service Dept.
49 W. 24 Street, 9th Floor, New York, NY 10010

Please send me the book(s) I have checked above. I am enclosing
$_____ (please add $1.00 to cover postage and handling).
Send check or money order only—no cash or C.O.D.'s.

Mr./Mrs./Miss _____
Address _____
City _____ State/Zip _____
Please allow six weeks for delivery. Prices subject to change without notice.

NEXT STOP:
SPACE STATION

". . . I am directing NASA to develop a permanently manned Space Station, and to do it within a decade." . . . President Ronald Reagan, State of the Union message, January 25, 1984.

Are you a person of vision? Are you excited about this next new stepping stone in mankind's future? Did you know that there is a magazine that covers these developments better than any other? Did you know that there is a non-profit public interest organization, founded by famed space pioneer Dr. Wernher von Braun, that actively supports all aspects of a strong U.S. space program? That organization is the NATIONAL SPACE INSTITUTE. If you're a member, here's what you'll get:

- 12 big issues of Space World magazine. Tops in the field. Follow the political, social and technological aspects of all Space Station developments—and all other space exploration and development too!
- VIP package tours to Kennedy Space Center to watch a Space Shuttle launch—the thrill of a lifetime!
- Regional meetings and workshops—get to meet an astronaut!
- Exclusive Space Hotline and Dial-A-Shuttle services.
- Discounts on valuable space merchandise and books.
- and much, much more!

So if you are that person of vision, your eyes upon the future, excited about the adventure of space exploration, let us send you more information on how to join the NSI. Just fill in your name and address and our packet will be on its way. AND, we'll send you a FREE Space Shuttle Launch Schedule which is yours to keep whatever you decide to do!

Name _____

Address _____

City, State, & Zip _____

NATIONAL SPACE INSTITUTE
West Wing Suite 203
600 Maryland Avenue S.W.
Washington, D.C. 20024
(202) 484-1111